Author's Note

This story itself has been quite a challenge to say the least. It has gone through various changes and fluctuations within the novel itself. The first book I wrote and published; Immortals Book One: A Quest for Home, was a fantasy adventure novel filled with witty remarks, sarcastic jargon, sly moments, and heroic banter as three heroic characters went through weird and wacky events and meeting the strangest of characters. I love my first book and am currently working on the second novel which is set in Hell. The six book fantasy series inspired by the author Rick Riordian who wrote the Percy Jackson series, the Kane Chronicles and Heroes of Olympus series, is a wonderful adventure full of magic, medieval intrigue and colorful scenery full of Egyptian, Greek, and Norse mythology. Although, it is a good book, and am excited to eventually start back up on it, it is complete unrealistic to reality.

I have always been interested in the 1600s era, in which is the hierarchy of the Age of Sail on the seas, with pirates, outlaws, and adventure, and the Dutch East India Company. I've always been a history nut, and I used to only prefer the 1800s era. Recently, my father had given me a book called Birds of Prey by Wilbur Smith, and it was set in 1667, following the life of a captains son. After reading this, I instantly became hooked on the 1600s time period and wanted to create a story of my own set in this time piece.

There is something intriguing yet magical to me about the 1600s time period. The feeling of sailing on a big ship with a rusty crew and captain along the seas, with a musket, cutlass, exploring uncharted lands and countries, along with drinking ale in taverns, the strength in your back, the wind in your hair, and the adventure in your eyes on the salty ocean, really just interested me. Not to mention the music of lutes, accordions, flutes, and harps is a lovely message of sound to the ear.

So, I took it upon myself to come up with a lovely salty sea story full of pirates and adventure along the ocean. I thought about it a lot before even beginning to write it out and just formed the bare bones of the story. Then I decided to set it in 1678, the late 1600s when the Dutch East India Company was becoming the ruler of the European seas. Originally, I just wanted it to be a 93 page short story, and made a audiobook for the story afterwards. Then I thought to myself that, its' a great story full of wonderful characters and amazing descriptions and voyages, and felt it needed to be expanded and told more throughly. Talking back about my fantasy novel series, Immortals it's mainly a comedic, fantasy, magical adventure which isn't bad it's lovely full of funny moments, heart felt moments, and goofy transitional characters, along with a crazy cast of individuals. But after writing it and starting on the second story of the series, I wanted to write something, for one, more realistic, set further back in history, more dark, grim, serious, and the hardship of the life of a pirate and to not sugarcoat it like most movies or other books do. Let's face it, the true life of a pirate was difficult, and that is putting it lightly. A life of a pirate was full of diseases, battles, betray, death, enslavement, rights, sea storms, challenges, loss of loved ones, and much, much more. I wanted to create a world that is colorful and magical but also make the story have this dark, gothic, fashionable style to it.

So, now we are here. I decided to make it into a 3 part series, along with a fourth addition that is separate from this book, which is a prequel to The Siren's Call.

I truly hope you enjoy this story, I have worked really hard on this forming the characters, the setting, the world and environment, and weaving the mystical blue depths through history correctly.

There is no other reason in saying this, but that just pirates are flat out awesome. So, I surely hope this wrenching salty sea tale on the seven high seas takes you across the world of Europe, Asia, Africa, and the Caribbean in the shoes of a English pirate, and that you get enveloped in the world of the 1600s.

Now, without further due my good people, The Siren's Call!

The Dutch East India Company Sigil and Headquarters

The Dutch East India Company

T'OOST INDISCHE MAGAZYN EN SCHEEPS-TIMMER-WERF.

Here are some definitions, terms, and phrases you will come across in the story. This is just to help you understand what they mean instead of having to look it up.

Letter of Marque

A letter of marque and reprisal (French *lettre de marque; lettre de course*) was a government license in the Age of Sail that authorized a private person, known as a privateer or corsair to attack and capture vessels of a nation at war with the issuer. Once captured, the privateer could then bring the case of that prize before their own admiralty court for condemnation and transfer of ownership to the privateer. A letter of marque and reprisal would include permission to cross an international border to effect a reprisal (take some action against an attack or injury) and was authorized by an issuing jurisdiction to conduct reprisal operations outside its borders.

Terms Used in the Book and Their Meanings

Ship Parts and Directions:

Ship-A large wooden vessel that is used to sail on the ocean from one location to the other lined with cloth sails.

Mainmast-the center wooden pole of the ship that holds it together, with rigged sails and rope. That is what pushes the ship forward using the wind to blow into the sail.

Wheel-the wheel of the ship, the piece of wood that steers the boat

Foremast-the mast of a ship nearest the bow

Mizzen mast-Smallest mast on the ship

Quarter deck-The part of a ship's upper deck near the stern, traditionally reserved for officers.

Shrouds-Ropes and yards of webbed rope that is wrapped around the masts and up through the sails for sailors to climb up to the nest or sails

Crows Nest-A circular wooden platform on the top of the main mast where a person can sit and get a view of whats ahead

Captains cabin-the room under the deck of the ship where the captain stays

Rudder-a flat piece hinged vertically near the stern of a boat or ship for steering

Chains-The chains were small platforms, built on either side of the hull of a ship, used to provide a wide purchase for the shrouds, and to assist in the practice of depth sounding.

Anchor- big iron contraption shaped like a hook that is attached to a chain that grabs the sea bed for the ship to stop

Gunport- an opening (as in a ship's side, a gun turret, a pillbox, or the nose, fuselage, or wing of an airplane) through which a gun can be fired.

Hull-under belly of a ship

Keel-front of the ship

Fore speak or beak-A section of a ship hold is within the angle of the bow for trimming, or sometimes used for storage of cargo

Figurehead-the front part of the ship where the ships symbol is bestowed, as such as a mermaid, or woman, or dolphin, or man made out of wood sits.

Fo'c'sle-The front deck

Deck-Open main deck in the center of the ship

Bow-spirit-a spar extending forward from a ship's bow, to which the forestays are fastened.

Jibboom- a small wood pole that supports rigging

Charts-maps filled with longitudes and latitudes that the captain would use to guide

Weaponry:

Musket Rifle-A musket is a muzzle-loaded long gun that appeared as a smoothbore weapon in the early 16th century, at first as a heavier variant of the arquebus, capable of penetrating heavy armor.

Blunderbuss-A big type of shotgun that sprays lead balls in a multiple directions, very deadly and roars loudly

GunPowder-a black grain that is used to ignite flames and guns

Flintlock pistol- A small wooden polished pistol, smaller version of a musket with a big cock arm, and bellowed muzzle

Cutlass-a longsword with a round hilt

Dagger- medium sized knife usually with gilded hilts

English Longbow- a big bow and arrow used for long range sniping with arrowheads

Culverins- another word for canon, which is a big black iron gun filled with canon balls to smash and damage ships

Mallet- a small hammer

Marlinspike- a small welded tool with a wooden shaft and circular lead ball on top with spikes

Double Swivel- a two barreled canon that is medium sized meant to fire out chained together canon balls

Falconet- a smaller canon shaped like a large blunderbuss to fire smaller canon balls and musket ball shrapnel

Torture Devices (For Act 3 of the Story)

The rack- a contraption that is a long wooden flat platform to where a human is laid on their back, tied with their hands and feet and is "racked" and their labs stretched out till the break

Bronze Bull- a bronze cooker shaped like a bull, to where lava is poured inside to where a human is cooked alive inside

Thumbscrews- The device consisted of three upright metal bars, between which the thumbs were placed. A wooden bar slid down along the metal bars, pressing the thumbs against the bottom. A screw pressed the wood bar downward, crushing the thumbs painfully. The thumbscrews were an elaboration of an earlier device known as the pilliwinks, which could crush all 10 fingers and resembled a nutcracker.

The Wheel-The victim would be tied to the wheel, and then swung across some undesirable thing below -- fire was always a good choice, but dragging the victim's flesh across metal spikes also worked well. The wheel itself could also have spikes mounted on it, so the pain came from all directions. Instead of swinging, the wheel might turn on an axle. The difference was likely immaterial.

Burning at the stake-tying a human to a wooden pole and burning them alive

The Pillory-a wooden holding to where a human was embarrassed and laughed at in the towns square with their head and hands in a pole

The Iron Maiden- Similar to the bronze bull, people where placed inside a iron cell and spikes impaled them from the inside
Rat Torture- A lantern of light was placed on a person stomach and a rat would bury itself into the persons stomach

The Anguish- a iron hook would by stabbed into a man's spine and them tightened until the person was forced into a slumped position

The Saw- a person is hanged upside down and sawed through the anus and stopped at their belly to bleed out while they are still alive

Currency:

Pence: a type of penny

Gold Coin or
 deplume-a golden coin used as money back in this era

Silver coin- a silver coin that was cheaper than a golden coin by half

Religion

A pulpit - a raised platform or lectern in a church or chapel from which the preacher delivers a sermon.

Priory-a church

Vestry- offices where the priest works

Nunnery- a house of nuns

Monastery- a house for monks

Drink

Ale- a type of beer or mead, typically thicker than regular beer

Rum- a liquor that consists of gold, white, red, or black

Millet Mead- a type of beet fermented from wheat and wild honey

Sea Creatures Mythical and Realistic:

Mermaid or Siren- a mythical half woman, half fish who would lure sailors to their death by song and love

Kracken- a giant squid known for sinking ships

Water Nymphs-a druid water creature that plays a harp

Davy Jones- captain of the Flying Dutchman, who hunts souls of the damned across the seas, captain of the dead

The Flying Dutchman- Davy Jones ghost ship

Sailor Slang

Sea going- meaning glad to be arriving in port

Captain-the leader and commander of the vessel

First Mate- second in command, closest men to the captain

Port- a place or location to dock a ship and grab supplies and rest

Cargo-supplies carried on a ship

Crewmen- the crew of the captain

Mutiny- when the crew over throws the captain and second in command or whoever is most powerful takes the over as captain

Cables Length- word for a mile long or a few miles long

Cartographer or Navigator- the man who reads the charts and maps on the ship and directs the captain

Laddie- a man or best friend

Lassie- a woman

Whorehouse or Brothel- a house that holds women explicitly prosecuting their bodies sexually to men or women, a house of sex

Sea dog- another word for a sailor

Mariner- another world for a sailor

Seafarer- a man who loves the sea

Helmsman- the man who steers the ship, but the captain sometimes steer it also

Coxswain- a sailor who is in charge of the crew

Deckhand- crew who performs manual duties

Landlubber- a fool or clumsy person

Scallawag- a man who is a ruffian or pirate

Limejuicer- a British ship

Swab the deck-clean the deck

Run up those guns- load the canons

Let her taste our iron-fire on a enemy ship with canons

Yellow belly- a fool, or bastard

Jack tar- another word for a sailor

Gob- a bump or cut

Sultan- a leader of a country, usually in command of a army

Earl- Leader of said port, or country

Duke- second in command to the Earl

Tie that rigging- tie the rope tight

Steer her portside- steer her left

Steer her starboard- towards the stars, which is right

Straight bow- sail straight ahead

Cheese-heads- another word for a Dutch soldier of Dutchman

Give me my effects- Give me my things or items

Cabin boy- the sailor or young man who keeps the under deck in check

Cargo supplier or holder- the man who checks the cargo and makes sure its secure

Let her fly out or give sail away or beat her to the tack- let the sail fly and give it wind

Corsair- another word for pirate

Privateer- a sailor who sails under a Letter of Marque under the Majesty's command and security

Table of Contents

Map of the World- 17th Century Era

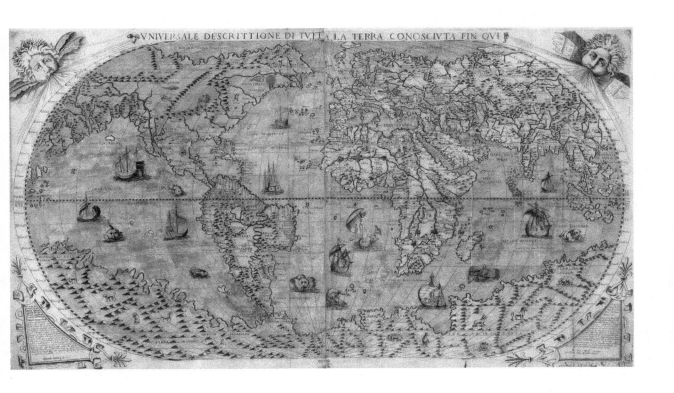

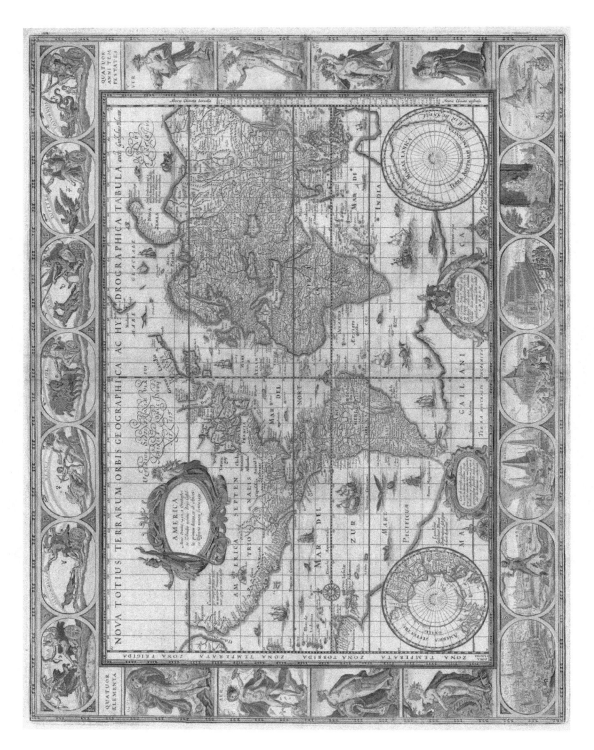

NOVA TOTIUS TERRARUM ORBIS GEOGRAPHICA AC HYDROGRAPHICA TABULA auct. Judocho Hondio

Dedication

To my girlfriend Yari Cintron, who continuously inspired me to write this story, and expand it just by her being interested and enjoying to sea tale on its own. Thank you for the constant support throughout this writing process all the way up to getting it published into a book series. She provides unlimited care, love, and support for my writing career and I couldn't be more happier to have her in my life, she is an amazing person. This is for you baby, I love you.

The Siren's Call

Act 1: The Beginning of a New Adventure

For any reader who enjoys a wrenching salty sea tale along the seven high seas. Slip on that cap, tighten your cutlass to your belt, load that musket, chug back a swig of ale, and embark into the world of pirates my friend.

Part I

A New Voyage

September, 1678
London, England

The ship was docked at the bay just off the coast of London. It's white sails pasted onto the tall beams of the mast, the ropes looking like yellow coiled snakes strapping and wrapping across her white blankets. The wind blew strong and fast against the sails making them puff out towards the sea ahead. The side of the ship was painted anew, with blue and gold streaks of oil paint dazzling in the sunlight. The hull of the ship creaked and groaned, as the timbers popped and corked under the teal waves of the deep blue.

I rested against the rim of the ship on the right gazing out towards the city of London. With its bustling trade ports, high churches and monk monasteries, cobblestoned streets, bakery shops, pubs, whorehouses, and tile and brick houses, it gave me a sense of home of the like. I looked back out towards the endless abyss of the ocean. I shivered seeing that cold pit of blue, but it also excited me to be going on the voyage with a lively crew of mates. London is not in the greatest conditions at the moment but, it still is my home.

The London tower cranked out a loud bell ring, that echoed through the village square all the way up to my ears on the ship.

I peered at the golden tower, above all other buildings gleaming in the light. At this time, most people would be attending mass. I knew it was an unworthy act of God to miss mass at the time, but we had uncharted waters to explore. The ship I was sailing on what called the Deloraine. Named after the queen of Norway back in the 1450s, she's a fast runner, and can go up against high waves and coral reefs that may damage the crusted barnacled under hull, that after being, submerged for a long period of time, is home to mussels, crabs, barnacles, and squid.

The Deloraine was famous in the British Isles and along the seven high seas. She had been in many scraps and battles over the years but she's held her own.

As the salty air of the ocean water shot up my nose, and the green seaweed swayed under the waves in a mangled twisty form as if they were vines, I had a nudge at my left shoulder that almost made me topple over the side of the ship.

"What you doing gawking at that seaweed for? Get on up, and help me tie these here crates to the rigging." A male voice shot out at me.

I looked to my left to see it was my friend Daniel Ogsworth. Daniel was a strong man, with a tense look on his face all the time but he always knows when to set things straight. He's been in many battles, and has been to a few other lands that I haven't been to yet. Knowing that, to me he was a legend and I looked up to him. Daniel was a few years older than me being 35, and me being only 26 I looked up to the man.

His long black shaggy locks hung down to his shoulders, drenched in sweat from lifting big crates up the long wooden beams that lead to the ship deck. His white face was as red as a tomato from working.

"Henry, don't make me repeat myself. Get a move on son." He said to me like I was his son and he was the father.

I nodded and began to pull away from the rim until I heard a whistle. I spun back towards the docks to see a few women in colorful dresses whistling at me and winking. Most of the women had provocative dresses on, with big breasts, showing the long smooth legs. I felt myself get excited and felt my penis engorge inside my breeches. I bit my lip softly to myself, lusting for a women's touch. It had been quite a while since I had a women's touch to my skin. They continued to whistle at me.

I noticed my brown breeches, the front part was poking out, but they couldn't see that because the ships wooden hull rim was blocking it. My white ruffled v necked shirt was unbuttoned a little showing my white chest. My long brown hair danced by my shoulders, and my hazel eyes darted from one lady to the next wanting them.

"Come on down and will show you a good time big boy." One woman grinned up at me.

"Yes, please, We insist." Another moaned.

I started to lean over the edge but Daniel caught the back of my neck collar. He yanked me backwards and spun me around.

"No need for that." He muttered. He looked down at my breeches poking out.

"God damn Henry. No need for that at all. We have a voyage to go on."

"Even though, we are just delivering shipments of crates full of sugar, spices, bronze, iron, grapeshot, and paper?" I snickered.

Daniel cracked a hearty laugh. "Boy, indeed, but we will be paid well in gold and coin. Not only will we be rich men by the end of this voyage, we will get two explore unknown islands, and lands unlike any other. We get the experience."

"The experience?" I asked him.

Daniel snickered and set the crate full of rice grains down next to him and leaned his right elbow on it making his body slanted.

"Yes lad. Think of all the women we will encounter mate! Not only that, but the battles we will engage in over the seas." Daniel heroically smiled.

"You must be right." I smiled.

"I'm always right. Also," Daniel picked up the crate and pointed at my half enlarged penis. "Don't think with that." Then he pointed to his head.

"Think with this, it'll get you farther in life."

He turned to look back out to the city of London for a minute and back at me. He smiled a row of yellowed teeth. He tossed me the crate. I barely caught it stumbling down onto my ass. The crate toppled to my right almost spilling out the contents of rice. Daniel cracked a high pitched laugh.

"Lad, you can't catch a crate." He slapped his knee.

I groaned and gripped the crate as some other sailors snickered at me as well. I shrugged it off and grinned slyly at Dan.

"Fuck ya you damn blunt." I smiled.

"Fuck ya too Henry." Daniel laughed.

I smiled as I passed him and walked over and shoved the big wooden crate into the bundle of crates attached into the big rope swing.

The sailors yelled cranking the rutters up pulling the crates high into the sky above. Water from the sea dripped from the bottom of the crates and bounced on my long brown hair.

Within a hour, we set sail. The mast were pulled, the ropes unattached from the wooden poles on the sides of the ship, the white sail blew in strong mighty wind, pushing the boat into the waters. I looked back at the city of London giving it a wave goodbye. I looked back the sea, seeing the endless blue ahead of me. I peered up at the wheelhouse seeing Captain Samuel, steering the mighty beast into the unknown. His big white beard blowing in wind, his black flat hat on top of his head followed with his big black trench coat swaying below his boots. I didn't know much about the captain other than he was a tough son of a bitch. I'm glad we are sailing with him and we hopefully were in good hands.

The boat churned in the waters, making the boat sway to the right. I grinned so widely as much as a man could grin. I sprinted to the head of the ship, gripping the top of the mast port pole. I gazed past my boots to see the waves mashing up against the hull creating a white ruffle, until it dipped back into the deep blue.

On the front of the Delatroin sat a mermaid, made of wood. Her breasts big, her stomach flat, her face gorgeous and expressionless, her tail curling around the front of the ship. I never believed in the legend of the sirens and I was told by my father too beware of them, for they lure sailors to their death with their melodies. I thought it was fool hearty, not real at all.

I peered back at the front of the ocean getting closer and closer ahead. Dolphins of gray sleek skin and emerald eyes swam under the hull. The creatures jumped out of the waters and flipped in the air doing flips and twirls squeaking and chirping at us. I was surprised that they could keep up faster than the running teal ship and not get crushed under her bottom, but their boney flat tails were keeping up fast. Their dorsal fins cut through the water creating a straight line in the water. Their two small nostrils on their pointy noses blew steam from their craters. Such beautiful creatures. I laughed loudly over the blowing salty wind spraying water into my face making it feel cool from the humid air above.

I glanced behind me to see the black iron cannons strapped down on either side of the ships, tied by tight ropes. Canon balls were stacked in pyramids next to them glazed with oil and butter to make them slid smoother into the hole of the explosive contraption.

I watched other sailors climb the ropes that looked more like spider webbed up to the crows nest. I man sat watching in the crows nest, peering through white telescope at the sea.

The other sailors climbed the tangled mess of rope and tackle, balancing above high on the beams of the masts with the white blankets blowing close to them. I gulped knowing I would have to do that soon at some point, and losing my balance on that would be death for sure.

Other sailors were tightening the ropes on the canons, while others san across the deck carrying barrels of muskets, grapeshot, powder flasks, and flint and steel all over the front and lower decks. The brown guns jingled against each other in the barrel as they went past. Another sailor was carrying a blunder buss, with a big opened barrel, the blunder buss was a strong powerful gun.The blunderbuss was the type of firearm with a short, large caliber barrel which is flared at the muzzle and frequently throughout the entire bore, and used with shot and other projectiles of relevant quantity and/or caliber. It was mostly used in short range combat while the musket offered a longer range of attack.

After looking at the gun, I saw Daniel laughing his way, passing through the crew men. I looked at the captain gazing at his charts and maps to guide us through the rough waters.

Daniel clapped my right shoulder and stood next to me looking out at the sea. "Ready for Sweden?" He smiled.

"Of course. I've heard many stories of bakeries and unbelievable delicious pastries and chocolate fancies. I've heard there are bakeries on every corner and the food is extravagant." I smiled greedily ready to taste the food of that country.

I knew our trip would take atlas two years. We were going from England, to Sweden, to Norway, to Ireland, to Germany, to Madagascar, and then we'd loop back through the Horn of Africa and cut through India back to England. Sweden was our first stop to drop most of the supplies to the Duke of Sweden of Javar.

Daniel handed me a quarter full of a whiskey bottle full of Markers whiskey. The whiskey was the color of bronze with a tint of red in the liquid.

"Why only a quarter full of the bottle?" I asked confused.

"Cause laddie, we can't get to drunk, we gotta man the port side." Daniel crackled a deep baritone laugh that echoed through the ocean, and I was for sure every manner of creature in the deep blue could hear it.

Daniel swung his arm around my neck gladly. I eyed the bottle. It was glass, half full of the whiskey. I took a gulp feeling it sizzle and burn down my throat. I coughed a bit, feeling my eyes water and sting from the intense sensation of the burning liquor. I grinned slightly at Dan, who grinned back. He took the bottle from me and finished it off, wiping his mouth and tossing the glass bottle overboard into the waves. The bottle was swooped up into the white ruffle. I blinked to clear the tears from my eyes. Captain Samuel yelled from the wheel house.

"Get to work you bloody wankers!" Samuel croaked a raspy voice at us.

I gave him a wave and trotted over to the left side of the ship. I checked the ropes that were batting down the canons. The canons seemed secure enough so I ran over to the right side and check the barrels of guns. As I did this, Daniel ran below deck.

I checked the barrel of muskets. Their stocks high, there brown stocks, silver barrels, and metal triggers all gleaming in the breezy air. The grapeshot of the musket ball sat in boxes next to the wooden barrel. Black gunpowder sat in bull horn flasks, little black grains of pepper filled it up to the top.

"How many muskets are in the barrel Master Henry?" A sailor called out from the starboard bow. The sailor trotted over.

He was a stout young man, a little younger than me. Maybe early twenties. He had long blonde hair tied in a bun with a thread. He had light hair under his chin, and I could tell he wasn't able to grow a full beard yet. He smiled a wide grin at me, seeing him a younger lad than me, he was surprised to be asking me such a question but I didn't mind.

"What's your name?" I asked him.

"Timothy McGaw sir. I like to be called Tim instead sir." The boy responded fast in a high pitched voice.

"Nice to meet you. Henry HeartStone. How old are you son?" I asked Timothy.

"I turned 20 earlier this May sir." Tim smiled.

"Cut the sir's out I'm only 26. Pleasure to be aquatinted." I smiled.

"Same as well. Again, Master Henry, how many muskets in the barrel? I need to take stock for the winter. It comes soon." Tim said.

I scanned the barrel of guns counting with my eyes. I turned back to him.

"32 muskets Master Timothy." I said.

Tim scribbled down on a scribe scroll and rolled it up and tucked it under his arm. "Thank you." Tim nodded.

I smiled at the young man. "Of course. It is my pleasure."

"What do the other barrels count for?" Tim asked me more seriously.

I eyed up the wheelhouse to see Captain Samuel staring at his compass. He veered the big boat towards East, as I felt her sway under my feet, and head into the sun. The sun beaded down on all of us, creating heat.

"Well, let's see." I said.

I walked around the other wooden barrels as young Tim trailed behind me, scribbling on his paper with a feathered pen. I eyed two barrels of muskets.

"These two barrels count 23 each of muskets." I said and then pointed to the blunder busses. "87 blunder buss in this barrel, and the other holds...it holds..." as I peered into the barrel, "103."

Tim scribbled down the numbers I had presented him. "Perfect."

"What else needs to be counted for?" I questioned the man.

"Powder and shot." He reasoned quickly.

I looked at Tim seeing sweat trickle down his face. He ushered me too count the powder.

I looked at the powder flasks, and grapeshot, musket shot, and canon balls. "10 pounds of cannon ball. 100 pound of powder and black grain, also 45 pounds of lead shot and grape." I said.

"All well. Thank you Henry. I will report the markings to Samuel to let him know we are stocked well for if we encounter a battle of some sort." Tim smiled.

I watched the man hurry past me and up the stairs to the Captain. He quickly showed the counts of the guns and powder to Samuel. The captain nodded with approval. Daniel suddenly came up beside me.

"Below deck is hotter than a woman's skirt above her waist." He giggled. "The canons seemed to be strapped under the deck."

"You double checked the rigging?" I asked him.

"Course I did you savvy. I always double check." He grinned.

"How long do you think it'll take us to get to Sweden?" I wondered.

"A month or two. Then soon we'll drop off the supplies and be drinking white rum on the shores." His eyes danced with amusement.

"Mhm, white rum, black rum, gold, and red, sounds like a dream right now." I licked my lips for the savory drink.

"Once we get paid lad, we will get all the rum, and all the women we want." Daniel danced a little jig swinging his legs in and out from under him.

I laughed and did the same placing my hands on my sides and kicked my legs out in front of me, one after the other. Daniel laughed a strong bellow from his belly. Daniel lifted his hands in the air.

"Gents, we are one are way to Sweden!" Daniel croaked happily.

All the group of the crew cheered happily, whistling and yelling for drink and women to be what we were heading for, and not only that but real adventure. My heart was filled with excitement for this voyage, for the lands I will get to see one explore, the people I'll meet, and the cultures I'll learn and embrace. The battles will fight and win. This was the first real voyage I had ever been on in my life, so the thrill of the unknown filled my body with delight.

Sailors all around carried barrels around taking them below and above the quarter and poop decks. Men climbed the ropes and nests, letting out the sails to give it room to breathe and letting the wind catch her fast and hard.

The ship lurched forward at surprising speed, gunning towards the horizon. Daniel cleared his mouth and began to sing a wonderful song called Roll the Old Chariot. This was a familiar sea shanty my father would sing whenever he was home.

"Oh will be alright if the wind was in our sails!" Dan cried happily. Immediately, the whole crew began to join in twirling around dancing hearty jigs and rigs. People sang it, whistled, danced, and yelled it, and I began to sing along. Daniel started to sing the main lyrics first and then the whole crew joined in all together in one big yell from our hearts. Me and Daniel danced clasping hands and swung in circles. People clapped their hands loudly, and stomped their feet against the wooden planks smiling with adventure in their eyes. We were all men ready for the waters, and for adventure and excitement of this trip. Even the Captain whistled along with us with a slight grin under his cap.

As we sang, our work seemed to become more and more passionate and we worked harder in the heat. The sun shone down on us, scolding our necks and backs, turning it bright red, but we didn't care, we were full of joy. The crew scrubbed the planks with soap and water with fat brushes attached to black handles. The straw brushes rubbed on the planks getting rid of the spilled over oil and loose nails and dust. Other sailors ran across the deck, four men lifting and carrying a mini two barrel canon and began to attached it to the side of the ship, pulling chains and lead strings to the wood. I followed Daniel who tossed me a brush and we began to scrub the planks under my feet until it shown clean and bright. I sat up ready for Sweden. I peered out beyond the rim of the ship, out into the ocean, seeing London was now just a speck in the water.

November
Javar, Sweden

As I lay under my hammock, it rocking back and forth under the movement of the ocean waves, I was tired and sleepy. The night before was a long hard working night, lifting heavy iron rods up through the main mast to keep it steady.

The Delatrone creaked under the blue, its timbers riveting against the water and rotting wood combining and smashing together. We had been traveling for a little over two months on this ship and with this crew and we haven't lost a soul yet. We were making good time, delivering our supplies to Javar. All our supplies full of sugar, spices, rice, wheat, grains, iron, lead, gunpowder, muskets, musket balls, cinnamon, lavender, honey, coffee, and ale and much more were all stocked and accounted for.

Along our travels through the treacherous waters of Poseidon's deep blue, we didn't encounter a single friendly ship or an enemy which was wonderful. The entire two months of traveling towards Sweden, I couldn't wait for the sweets that await me. Every day that passed, was closer to the bakeries and lovely chocolates of that city.

Just as I was thinking about it Daniel rushed down the poop deck, almost tripping down the wooden stairs. He had an intense expression on his face that I couldn't understand but it soon broke into a smile.

He gripped the side of my hammock knocking me off, making me topple onto the planks with a thud.

"Ow, shit, Daniel. What is make of all this noise?" I shot at him.

"Henry my boy! We have arrived!" Daniel smiled brightly.

"Arrived?" I asked him.

"In Sweden! Come to the deck!" He shouted.

I hopped up and followed him, up the stairs onto the quarter deck. I rushed to the edge of the boat. I looked behind me to see the captain steering us into the port at the docks. The bell rang in the distance and I could hear people bustling around as we pulled in closer to lay anchor.

"Look at that lad." Daniel smiled widely at the city.

I followed Daniels eyes to the town of Javar, Sweden. It was gorgeous. The wooden docks stretch towards the stone bricked stairs and walls, leading up into the city. Huge ships with multiple colored sails of black, red, white, and blue dotted the sides of the docks, swishing in the waves and rocking slightly under the momentum.

Many sailors and mates, were crowding the docks heading back to their boats ready to sail out again, or just getting off and stretching their sea legs.

I peered further into the city and could see tiny dots of humans bustling about, talking, shopping, eating, drinking, dancing, and laughing.

The crossroad itself looked sublime. With its birch wood rooftops, elm wood walls and vibrant, rare trees, Javar has a inviting atmosphere. I knew only little about this place, other than its glorious sweets, was it was known for its fishing and hunting of game.

Further into the town, I could see a giant building made of white marble, and a crystal blue rooftop.

Daniel nudged my arm. "That's the town hall. We gotta give the Duke of Javar our supplies before we can eat."

Tim hopped up next to us. "What a mighty city I say." His young green eyes gleamed at the magnificent township.

I patted his back. "Indeed my young man. Now, let's go see what it has in store for us."

Captain Samuel, jumped down from the wheel. The boat pushed forward slowly, lurching in the waves heading for the docks to be sat. He folded his map, tucking it in his trench coat pocket to his side. He slipped his compass into his pocket.

"Weigh anchor men!" He bellowed.

We all hurried across the deck and took hold of the wooden spinner laid in the center of the ship above iron bars on the floor. Me, Daniel, and five other men, heaved, screamed, and pushed the wheel in a circle. I gritted my teeth tightly grinding them against each other, my arm muscles bulging, feeling tired already, my blue veins popping above my skin, began to spin the contraption.

All six of us groaned shoving the wheel round and round. At first it was slow, but the wheel cranked and screeched as we started to spin faster and faster. Underneath my feet, I could hear, and feel the metal anchor fall from chain, and smash under the ocean waves. The boat was sailing closer to the docks. Finally, the anchor let way, and I stumbled back letting go. The wooden wheel creaked to a stop. I felt the anchor catch the bottom, and the ship creaked forward into the waves, swallowing the front woman of the ship halfway under water and then we popped back to safety next to the docks.

A few men hurried with a long wooden bridge. They slipped open a little wooden door, and slid the wooden plank downward, until it hit the docks. All the men, including me, were eager to rest after two months at sea, and hungry for some real food. Trust me, stew of potatoes and carrots, dry rye bread, beans, and dried meat get tiring everyday.

Captain Samuel held up his hand and faced his mighty crew of one hundred and thirty. His white beard stretching down to his chest, blew in the wind. His rough eyes darted across his crew fast.

"Now, I understand we are all eager to eat and relax for a few days. Trust me, I am too. This old legs get tired too." He smirked.

The whole crew laughed with him. The Captain held up his hand again, to silence our laughter.

"We will eat soon enough, we just have to get the crates of supplies down to the palace in the center of town to deliver to the Duke. Then we can drink all the rum, and eat all the sweets we want!" He cheered.

The crowd whistled and cheered happily. "Get those crates lads!"

Me, and Daniel, and Tim hurried down under the deck and began lifting up the various crates full of supplies. I lifted two crates of coffee beans, and one of black gunpowder. Daniel, had five balancing them on top of both his shoulders, his bugling arms pulsing in the sun.

Timothy stumbled upon the steps carrying a messily one crate. Multiple sailors ran back and forth lifting up crates from below deck and handing them to other sailors above. Even the captain carried two.

Daniel crackled a laugh at young Tim. "Only one Tim e'boy?"

Tim blushed slightly. "Yes sir. I can-"

Daniel shushed him. "Here you go me lad."

Daniel set two more wooden crates on top of Tim's one crate. Tim's arms began to shake a bit and he struggling to keep his balancing wobbling along the deck. Me and Daniel snickered with laughter, seeing the young mate struggle. I remember being his age and trying to figure out life and what not. I sympathy his position. The crew began to make their way down the wooden platform, carefully to not drop a crate into the water or to fall in themselves. Once my feet hit the stone ground, we jogged up the stone stairs and entered the town. Captain Samuel lead the way as the crew followed behind. The crates were blocking most of my view, so I didn't see much of the city as we passed through to the palace but I was okay with that, since we'd get to spend a few days there.

After a few miles we entered the courtyard of the palace. My arms were already feeling weak and sore from hiking these crates out. Tim had fallen a mile back and I had to help the young lad with one crate and take it for him. Daniel was just fine, carrying six crates on his shoulders.

The courtyard was beautiful with roses bushes, full of white, red, pink flowers, white greek marble statues, ponds, and fountains of old. Green jacketed guards with muskets stood guard on the corner with black caps, and green coats with gold buttons lining down their bellies.

The palace was massive with golden pillars on the outside, and marble floors. We carried the crates through double doors. As our boots clapped against the marble floor, it echoed through the hall. Slim braziers attached to each of the eight travertine columns light up the entire throne hall and cover the hall in warm oranges and dancing shadows. The paintings of angels and cherubs on the arched ceiling dance in the flickering light while memorials look down upon the stone floor of this regal hall.

A maroon rug runs from the throne down the center and loops back from both left and right while square dag banners with burnished sides decorate the walls. Between each banner hangs a small chandelier, they've all been lit and in turn illuminate the paintings of gods and goddesses below them.

Thick windows are hidden by veils colored the same maroon as the banners. The curtains have been adorned with burnished corners and intricate embroidery.

A towering throne of molten steel sits within a pagoda of sorts within this hall and is adjoined by three equally impressive seats for those aiding the royal highness in all affairs.

The throne is covered in tangled etchings and fixed on each of the slim ears is a carved sun. The fluffy pillows are a light maroon and these too have been adorned with gilded plumes.

Those waiting to see their royal highness can do so on the plethora of long and rather bulky alder benches, all of which are diagonally facing the throne. Those of higher standing can instead take seat in the embellished mezzanines overlooking the throne.

The Duke of Javar sat on the throne. He was fat, with a long stringy gray wig on top of his head, so I assumed he was bald under it. His beady eyes squinted at Captain Samuel and his crew as we placed the crates on the floor.

"Captain Samuel?" He softly asked.

"At your service sir. We have brought you the order you requested. All the way from London my lord.' Samuel smiled.

"Greeting, Captain Samuel. I understand you are apart of the order am I correct?" The man smiled, and his cheeks jiggled as he did so.

"Correct. I am with the Order of the Holy Knights Templar of his Great Majesty's Royal Naval Company, of England, behind the order and back up of Sir Francis." Captain Samuel smiled happily. He gestured to us. "These are my mighty crew of ruffians. There a bunch of rowdy mates but they get the job done."

"Welcome Samuel and his crew to Javar, Sweden. How long do you plan on staying before sailing off again?" The Duke smiled at him.

"A few days or so." Captain nodded.

"Wonderful. I'm sure you'll enjoy the food and drinks. You our under my protection good sir. Now, the supplies you brought me?" He slowly sat up to get a closer look at the crates.

Captain Samuel nodded to me and one other sailor. I walked over and pushed a crate closer so the Duke could see. I kicked off the wooden top revealing a box full of coffee beans and another full of barrels full of ale.

Captian Samuel pulled out a scroll from his coat. He unrolled it carefully and read it.

"5 pounds of coffee beans, 8 pounds of ale, 13 pounds of lead and paint, 45 pounds of powder, 23 pounds of rice, 12 pounds of tobacco, 2 pounds of iron, 32 pounds of musket ball, 78 pounds of cotton, 4 pounds of wheat, 14 pounds of spices, sugar, and so forth. There you have it as promised."

The Duke of Javar laughed happily. "You've done well Captain. Thank you for the delivery."

"Of course." The Captain smiled.

"Where our you off too next to deliver these wonderful supplements?" The Duke wondered.

"Norway. Which is why...." Samuel pulled out a piece of paper. He unrolled it and walked over to the Duke slowly. "We need your signature to pass through the Norwegian pass to get into the town to drop of these supplies."

The Duke sat back. "You know English pirates aren't welcome in that region?"

"I'm aware, that is why we need documentation from you. If they see it's from you, their ally, will be set fair." The Captain headed the man.

The Duke sat back thinking and put his fat thumb under his triple chin. He waved his hand impatiently. "Very well. Guard. A pen please."

Within a minute, a green jacketed guard, brought the Duke a black inky pen and a bottle of ink. He dripped the sharp golden end in the black ink and signed the signature on the paper, as Samuel held it open for him.

Once the signature was done, he waved his gold ring over a candle and put a red waxed stamp of the lion on the bottom of the paper and blew on the wet wax to dry it.

Samuel smiled and rolled it back up. "Thank you, your Lordship."

"My pleasure." The man smiled. He waved his hands for the guards to gather the crates and take them further back into the temple. "Now, go enjoy the town!"

Me and Daniel and Tim rushed down the cobbled road into the city as our crew swarmed the shops and bakeries. Passing by many townspeople, I ran into many different people. Civilians, women of beauty that would give us looks of pleasure and lust, slaves, other men from other lands, and much more. We walked into a bakery off the corner of a street called Gotunar. Inside was a impressive and delicious collections of sweet lined up behind a glass wall.

Behind the glass, were cinnamon sticks, chocolates, pastries with yellow and blue creams in the center, jelly filled, and blood oranges, and macaroons of pink and green. My mouth watered for the taste. The man behind the counter, wore a white cap and looked at us a bit oddly, probably because we were covered in sweat and dirt from and smelled of ocean. I pulled out a few shillings and tossed them to the man behind the counter. I selected a pastry filled with blue and yellow cream. He handed it to me and I bite into it and tasted the sweet tartness that I had been waiting for. The blue and yellow cream filled my mouth with such tart with a mixture of sugar and cream. My mouth was overcome with a sensation of sweetness and I smiled to myself. Daniel and Tim bought about ten pastries and devoured them in five minutes. "This is the most amazing thing I have ever put into my mouth." Tim smiled happily.

We spent the last few days eating luxuries and enjoying the drink of ale and eating devious meats of lamb and pork and devouring sweets like pastries and chocolates and cakes. Soon., Captain Samuel called us to the ship and we lifted the anchor and set sail for Norway.

December
Norway

Only a month had passed and Norway was already in view and the docks to make port was close. The air had gotten bitter and cold, whipping at our faces like a slap in the face. The snow flakes rained down from the sky, landing on our head giving us a light sleet of blanket in our hair.

My hair had gotten shagger now, and my beard firmer and more full on my face. Tim had gotten more buffer and slim, and Daniel seemed to look a little bit older.

"Lads, we made it to Norway!" A sailor screamed happily.

"Aye!" Everyone cried dancing happily.

I gripped the side of the left side of the boat and gazed out on the town of Norway. Even though, I was happy to be off the ship for a time, and away from the cold waters, the town or Bigvur, Norway looked cold and barren. Large fat cold stone gray mountains sat in the background of the town. Snow sat on the tips of the giant silent rocks. Snow flurries echoed down from the frozen clouds. As we sailed closer to the port, the men around me began to sing happily again despite the cold air around us. I wrapped my scarf around my neck to keep my skin warm, and pulled my black coat closer to my body. I closed my eyes and listened to the men around me sing the shanty. Daniel broke me out of the trance.

Daniel wrapped his arm around me. "Think of the women Henry! I've heard Norwegian women are the most gorgeous."

"What about our Brits?" I smiled.

"Oh, I need to get a little foreign every once in a while. Besides, we are going to be here for a month or so." Daniel smiled.

"Thank the Almighty. We need a rest and a place to rest from this winter." Tim shivered under his breath.

We sailed into port and the boat rubbed up against the docks. A few men let the anchor fall deep into the ocean. Once it hit bottom the quarter master yelled up to Captain Samuel who was gripping a scroll and pen. His white beard mixed with the snow flurries, seemed to be long down to his belly. His white long hair ran down halfway his back.

"45 fathoms and we hit the sandy!" The sailor hacked up to the captain. The captain scribbled it down and nodded to the sailor. I knew we were staying past Christmas here to try to avoid the cold. The Captain saw that it wasn't worth sailing through winter weather, we would get nowhere and most likely get frostbite and hypothermia.

Once the boat stopped we lifted the same crates we had brought to Sweden and delivered it to the high power. After that we settled down in a few Inn's through the month of December. The documentation signed by The Duke of Javar Sweden, got us through perfectly, although we had to argue with the guards about the right of passage further into the city. They thought we were trying to raid the city and held us under hold for a few hours but we managed to squeeze through thanks to the waxed documents.

We stayed mostly indoors to avoid the winter air, and the cold flurries raining down. After a week into staying here, I was already used to it. Ice had formed on the cobble stoned streets. Carriages could barely get through without the horses slipping under the hooves on the frozen ice. Edges of the roads were piled up under white snow blankets, and the roofs of the buildings were covered as well. Everyday the snow rained down, making the gray of the town more white.

Me, Daniel, and Tim stayed in a Inn just of Cranberry Street, only a few miles down the road was a tavern called The Eurgog. Same old same old happened. Supplies was delivered, and we received supplies in return. Much more gunpowder, guns, cannon balls, matches, lanterns, oil, and food and rum was being brought almost every 2 days or so to the Delatrone.

We had been in Norway for two weeks and now the winter was setting in hard. The snow began to get thicker and thicker outside. It piled and piled up more on the roads, now complete covering the stony ground. We would have to be completely covered up if we wanted to step outside without freezing to death. Many of our crew was scattered across the village of the town, in many Inns mainly staying in the pubs and food stands or whorehouses.

One night Me and Daniel decided to head to the tavern for a drink. Timothy decided to sleep in, he needed it. The young lad was working day and night lifting crates and cleaning the ships sides when the snow wasn't blowing to hard.

Me and Dan, excited our warm Inn and trailed down the snowy rode, covering our faces with our hands from a tiny blizzard that was beginning to nip at our faces. The hail was hitting our skin giving us pricks here and there. There wasn't many people out and about in the town since the weather was too cold. I watched my boots careful to try not to slip under the ice but my shoes would just sink three feet into the snowy powder and get my boots wet and cold. After a few minutes cutting through the dark oak buildings and lampposts on the sides of the town, we made it to the tavern. From the outside it looks cheerful, snug and peaceful. Plastered walls and well-crafted wooden beams make up most of the building's outer structure.

It's tough to see through the windows, but the enthusiastic noises from within can be felt outside. I gazed at the ships docked at the harbor, the boats shielded in ice and the bottom of the wood had begun to form icicles. The sails were rigged up and folded at the top of the masts.

As I entered the tavern through the well-crafted, metal door, me and Dan were welcomed by overall happiness and cheerful singing.

The bartender is swamped in work, but still manages to welcome me with a smile.

It's as engaging inside as it is on the outside. Several walls support the upper floor and the sconces attached to them. The walls are full of paintings, all in a different style, but all of the surrounding area..

The tavern itself is packed. Locals seem to be the primary clientele here, which often leads to exciting evenings. Several long tables are occupied by,

51

what seems to be the entire surrounding village. The other, smaller tables are also occupied by people who are indulging in great food and drinks, while some do try to strike a conversation, others can barely speak a word between eating what must be delicious food. Even most of the stools at the bar are occupied, though nobody seems to mind more company.

I recall hearing rumors about this tavern, supposedly it's famous for something,. Though judging by the amount of women in this tavern and the amount of them trying to subtly eye the bartender, it's probably his good looks and charm. I manage to find a seat and prepare for what will undoubtedly be a great evening.

Many of the people were speaking Norwegian in which I couldn't understand but Dan could understand, since he has been to Norway more than once.

A crackling red orange ember fire is ablaze in the fireplace in the back with two leather chairs next to it. I made a mental note to head there after we get our drinks.

The bar tender with a big black mustache across his face, smiled at me. He finished wiping down the counter and faced me and Dan.

"Hae, vigur a brundir se crek a koit?" (English Translation: What would you like to drink?) The bar tender asked me.

I blinked. "Uh what?"

Dan laughed and waved his hand at the bar tender. "You speak English?"

The bar tender looked at me and then Dan clueless. Daniel puckered his lip sourly. "Didn't think so. Pardon mi fruvir her, hie, Unnskyld min venn her, han snakker ikke engelsk." (Pardon my friend here, sir, He does not speak Norwegian.)

The bartender laughed loudly. I eyed both of them trying to figure out what they were saying.

The tender smiled widely. "Ikke en sak, kan du bare bestille for ham, hva vil det være?"

Daniel turned to me. I blinked at him. "What are you saying?"

"I told him you couldn't speak Norwegian. He laughed, and said it's alright. He's taking our order for drinks, what would you prefer?" Daniel asked me.

"Ask him what drinks do they have here?" I asked Daniel.

Daniel nodded and faced the bar tender. "Hva drikker har du her sir?" (What would you care for drink sir?)

The bar tender nobbed his head behind him to the pulleys. "Vi har jern ale, rum, whiskey, øl, gin...." (Ale, rum, wine, gin, whiskey...)

Daniel looked at me. "They have gin, ale, rum, wine, beer, of that such."

"I'd like a ale please." I smiled.

Daniel smiled. "Drek ol." (Ale please).

"Ogivur." (Great) The bartender smiled taking our shillings and stuffing it in his back pocket.

The bar tender grabbed two glasses and set them under the metal pulleys. He yanked them down, and brown liquid dark as the night, filled the rims of the glass until to foamed and frothed over the cup.

He slid the drinks to us. I took a swig and felt the cold tasty bitter beer travel down my throat and I smiled in satisfaction. I eyed the fireplace and nodded for Daniel to follow.

We walked over, and plopped down in the leather chairs. The warm burning fire felt nice against my clothes and body after being in the cold for so long.

Daniel and I drank in silence for a few minutes looking at the fire.

I felt the beer run down my throat and I noticed my drink was already halfway done and Daniel was almost on to a second one.

Finally, Daniel broke the silence. "Ireland is next. Dublin, Ireland."

"I know their ale is the best of the best. It's grandiose Dan." I smiled.

"Indeed. Yet, crossing into this channels, we will be encountering some Spanish fleets. More Naval ships." He frowned.

"Do we even have enough fire power for such a battle?" I asked him.

"I'm unsure." Daniel frowned.

"Well, from what I'm seeing, the path we keep traversing through, we will definitely encounter some enemy ships." I said.

We sat by the fire crackling away in silence again for a minute.

"Are you enjoying this voyage we are embarking on?" I asked Daniel.

Daniel sat back in his leather chair. He looked at me, and took a sip.

"All we are doing is delivering goods and trades to kings and mighty Dukes and Earls." I muttered.

"Your unhappy with?" Daniel asked.

"A bit aye." I muttered more under my breath to myself but Daniel heard anyway.

Daniel sighed and finished his drink. He frowned and sat his glass mug on the ground. He waved the bar tender over.

"Erg, fir rea shu en avgur shin yir." Daniel said to the barman, and slipped him two gold coins.

The bar tender nodded and hurried off. The bar tender went behind the counter and disappeared into the kitchen.

"What did you ask him to do?" I asked.

"I'm hungry. So I asked him to fetch us his best meal." Daniel smiled. "Also, black rum."

"Oh, thank you. Back to what I was saying, are you happy with this?" I asked him.

"As of right now, yes. Look, Henry, I know you are aching for some battle of a sort, but right now may be the only time we can truly relax for a time. We get women, drink, food, a place to sleep. Just embrace it while we have it." Daniel smiled.

I looked down at my boots, to the fire, and back at him. I was aching for a fight, I was getting sick of this constant trade and move from city to city with nothing exciting happening but then again we were traveling to some pretty interesting and vast towns that were beautiful.

"Your right." I smiled.

"I'm always right. Speaking of women, there's a beauty picking away behind ya." Daniel snickered.

I spun around in my leather chair to see a woman picking a lute. The lute was pretty enough, made from redwood. The string traveled up and down the shaft and the strings were clear and hard to see. Symbols of wolves and fire danced on the flat surface on the instrument, and the shaft was curved back and looked like it was bent at the top.

The woman picked the strings softly and began to sing. Her voice was like an angel. She sat on a wooden stool, and a small wooden cup of gold sat by her feet. She was beautiful, the most beautiful woman I had ever seen.

She had long red hair that flowed down to her lower back and it was straight and curly at the ends. Her eyes were blue like the ocean, her nose small and and freckles dotted her face. Her skin was white and smooth, and her lips fat and pink. Her breasts popped out from her white and brown woven dress shirt, with a loose brown leather thread keeping it held up and together. Her pants were brown and tight, and her boots had buckles on the end made of silver. Her hands moved with such movement and agility along the instrument it was hard to follow them. Her body was fine and curvy, hips wide, and body slim and slender.

She looked up from her lute and met my eyes. When she met my eyes, my eyes focused on her. I felt a pluck at my heart, a good pluck, like my heart wanted to leap out of my lips. I smiled at her, and she smiled back. Her smile was of another realm. It curved up the edge of her right cheek showing sparkling white teeth.

She kept her eyes on me for a time, and then began to sing. I couldn't recognize the song but her voice and words seemed to put me in a trance. It was like the world around me had stopped moving. Her voice swirled around my ears and body with such joy I felt so wonderful and full of light. Each line that she sung, she seemed to put true emotion behind it, as if she had lived this story she was singing.

I closed my eyes and listened to her entire song. Finally, when it ended, I had this big goofy grin on my face and Daniel was laughing at me which took me from the trance. I glared at him in irritation.

"What's so funny?" I barked at him.

"One, the food is here. So eat lad. Two, what's got you all jolly and burnt?" Daniel laughed.

I looked back at the singing woman. She finished her lyrics and the crowd of men and woman cheered for her. She smiled and a few people tossed her a few coins. After that, she began to pick the strings again. I looked back at Daniel.

"Oh, lad. A women can get a man's life twisted up in tangles and of the like." Daniel shot at me.

I eyed the beautiful woman again. She continued to pick the lute.

"You think?" I asked Daniel not even looking at him.

"Yes, I think so. Women are full of emotions and demand too much affection and jewelry of gold and silver and embroidery." He laughed.

I still didn't truly care. I thought she was beautiful, the most wonderful woman I have ever seen before my pupils. I gripped the side of the leather chair, watching the woman move her hair to her side, and strummed the instrument creating a light harmony that traveling through the tavern.

"I think she is magnificent." I smiled.

"Think of her what you like. I'm eating." Daniel snickered.

"Eating?" I asked.

I spun around to see the bar tender had delivered us the meal that was prepared back in the kitchen. The meal slapped my face with the smell, it shot up my nostrils with a warm meaty smell. On the china plate was cooked pork with rosemary and thyme laid on top the meat. A brown sauce was spilled over the delicate pig, dripping down the fatty parts. On the side of the plate was broiled seasoned potatoes of brown sugar and paprika and cayenne. Greens of seaweed laid flat and stringy next to it the smell of salt and vinegar. I licked my lips and smiled to myself. I picked up the knife and fork. Daniel licked his lips as well.

He licked his lips savory. "Henry my boy, we maybe messily shipmates, but tonight we eat like true kings."

My eyes danced with hunger for the meal. "You are right Daniel. Wish Tim was here to eat it with us."

As if on cue, Tim plopped down next to us. He picked up a potatoes from my shiny plate and popped it into his mouth, blowing on it as he chewed it fast.

"Aye, son, that was my starch." I croaked at him at little annoyed.

"Well, Henry sir, I was hungry." He laughed.

He snuggled up close to the orange fire. His long blonde hair, and white shirt was hung low. The woman picked the strings and and began to sing a song that my mother was familiar with when I was a child. The song the Willow maid was a lovely poem of a sorts talking about a lonely girl who lived deep in the forest in the willow who was trapped. Every man who fell in love with her couldn't break her free. She would sing it to me every night before I would sleep.

The woman sang it with such grace. As she sang, I focused on my meal. I cut into the meat, seeing the juice mix with the sauce. I stabbed the fork into the hearty dead beast, and shoveled it into my mouth. The flavors of rosemary, pepper, and swat vinegar stung my tongue with delight. I smiled wide and began to eat faster adding the greens and boiled potatoes along with the meat. Daniel took a few bites of his pleased, getting sauce all over the front of his shirt.

"You not sleeping well or something Tim me young boy?" Daniel laughed with a mouthful of greens.

"Not that. Just hungry and wanted a drink." He said taking a sip of his ale through a wooden mug.

"Here me lad." Daniel smiled.

He drove his sharp knife into the meat and and cut it in half and gave it to Tim who smiled and ate with us.

"Thank you." He smiled.

We all ate in silence enjoying the lovely meals of the tavern and drink. I chugged my ale down and recalled for another froth. I drank that with speed. The ale ran down my tongue with bitterness. As we eat, the woman continued her song.

Tim finally spoke up." So...Captain Samuel just got some more supplies to take to Dublin. Very interesting supplies."

"What kind of interesting supplies?" I asked curiously taking a bite of potatoes, feeling the purple redish skin peel off down my throat.

"Aye, what are you getting at Tim me lad?" Daniel letting his mug run dry, and called the tender over. "Erg vor." He said and slipped him some coins for a third.

The barkeep walked off to fetch Daniel a mug of rum this time. I looked at his eyes that were starting to turn watery and glassy.

"You sure you need more drink?" I questioned him.

He waved his hand at me. "Aye, more drink, more jolly."

I shrugged. I turned to Tim. "Tell me Master Tim, what cargo is Captain Samuel availed to you?"

"He has not availed of the such to my eyes. On the way to the tavern, I passed by a second tavern known as the Mystiske Kog-" I cut Tim off. Daniel set down his empty plate and bleached and the air of his beef breath hit my nose.

"What is the tavern called?" I asked Tim.

"The Mystique Kog?" He wondered.

"No, in English?" I curiously wanted to know.

"The Mysterious King. Anyhow, Tim, what supplies?" Daniel added.

"I saw Captain Samuel talking to a few gentlemen in the bar. I watched them for a good time, and they didn't see me at all. They handed Sir Samuel, a small wooden box. His back was facing me at this time, but he opened the box and I saw a lot of journals of the such but I was unsure because the frost was forming on the outer edges of the window sill." Tim continued.

"Timothy! Spying on the Captain is treason!" I whispered to him worried.

"Henry, now don't you go all fussing about and such. We won't speak of this to anyone." Daniel lowered his voice to low, and eyed the occupants of the tavern. No one was paying us attention.

"The journals looked old and woven from cow leather. Those are the most expensive type of booklets you could get." Tim noted.

The woman's lyrics still swirled around my ears in the background.

"It's seen as normal for a captain to have logs of our travels and to keep our supplies at dock." Daniel said not swayed by the suspicion.

"Why would he need cow leather, and also he could have just gotten horse leather which is cheaper and just as useful." I said.

"He is captain." Daniel noted.

"Aye, correct Sir Daniel, but not only was the journals suspicious, Captain Samuel had a crazy look in his eyes and was wary of the people around him.

58

He hurried out of the tavern and headed for the docked ship in the frozen bay." Tim said.

"Odd. We can keep an eye on him." I said.

"Indeed. Now gents, I'll be getting myself another ale." Tim smiled and hopped up from the warm fire, walking over to the bar keep to order.

The woman had finished singing, and was gathering her instruments. She collected the tiny amount of coins and slipped them in her pants. As Tim was ordering, he was having a hard time discussing drink matters with the bar keep, since Daniel was the only soul we knew that could speak Norwegian.

"I better go help the little lad out. Your lady is leaving, you better catch her." He cackled as he stood up and hurried over to the counter to help poor Tim out with the language.

I looked back at the small wooden table, glowing out of shadow in the firelight from the hearth. Sitting on top of the table, was a small bag of gold coins. I grinned to myself and looked back to Daniel and Tim laughing with the barkeep. I snatched up the gold coins in my hand and felt them swirl in the bag and cling together inside the pouch. I stuffed it into my pocket and stood up pushing my plate to the table. The meal was extravagant and my belly happily full, I turned to see the lady heading towards the doubled door. I rushed across the tavern, shimming through packed tables, laughter of gents and ladies over drink and banter, food being eaten, and cards being played. Music twiddled through the tavern. I sprinted across the tavern and I could feel some eyes on my neck but I didn't care. I made it to the door just before the red haired lassie exited.

"Wait uh!-" I shouted without thinking and with hesitation.

The beautiful maid spun around looking at me with a confused look.

"Um, do I know you sir?" The lady asked me. Her emerald eyes squinted at me with such intent.

"Uh, well, no madam. I would like to buy you a drink." I smiled ushering to the counter.

What are these feelings that plague me so? My heart felt fluttery, my stomach was in knots, my head was blank and dead, my eyes couldn't move from her figure. I couldn't understand these emotions but I liked them.

"A drink?" She asked me seemingly even more confused at my offer.

"Yes." I said.

She peered outside the window covered in white frost and snow flurries. The yellow sun starting to dip down below the blue horizon making the sky a pink orange haze over the white tundra.

It was getting dark out. "I was about to travel back to my home, I'm quite tired from playing the lute all day long." She said holding up the lute to my face.

"Well, how about just one drink?" I begged. What was I saying? Just her looks were getting to me, I couldn't control my feelings or what I was saying. I was sure she was going to laugh in my face and leave but instead she smiled at me.

"Alright. I wouldn't mind a drink." She pulled out only one gold shilling.

"But I don't have enough for a-" I snatched out the bag of gold coins and tinkled them in her face.

"Okay then." She smiled eyeing me with what I could see was interest of me now.

Daniel and Tim had a few more drinks eyeing me occasionally with the girl but they eventually left. I had gotten us both red rum, and we sat by the fire drinking across from each other. We didn't really speak at first, just drank rum, our eyes becoming glassy. Her lute was at the side of the chair and she was laying back in the chair enjoying her cup. I took another sip and set it down on the table.

"It's been a while since the last time I have had such a rest." She smiled.

"Thank you, the fire feels so warm. It's better than the winter cold outside."

"My pleasure my lady." I smiled.

She took a sip, and her eyes peered at me just over the rim of her mug with lust and affection.

"What's your name sailor?" She asked me curiously setting her cup down on the table next to mine.

"Henry HeartStone. Yourself?" I asked.

She gazed at me with emerald eyes. "Brita Haugen."

"So, your Norwegian but you can speak English well?" I curiously wondered.

"My father was an English merchant and my mother a Norwegian pub owner." She smiled. "I can tell you from England."

"The accent?" I asked.

"A easy pick." She smiled.

"You've been in Norway you're whole life?" I asked her taking another sip.

"Yes, I have not traveled anywhere else. Why are you here? Who are you traveling with?" Brita wondered.

"I have been in England my whole life and this is the first time I am traveling to other places with fellow sailors and crew mates. We under the command of Captain Samuel of the Holy Knights Templar of his Great Majesty's Royal Naval Company, of England, behind the order and back up of Sir Francis. We are delivering shipments of supplies to various countries and Norway is one of our stops." I told Brita.

"My goodness, where are you off too next after Norway?" Brita asked me.

"Dublin. We have to drop off a few more supplies before heading through Germany." I said.

"I wish I could travel that much in a set amount of time." Brita frowned to herself taking a sip of the ale.

"Wish I could take you." I smiled.

She slightly smiled to that response. She then looked at me. "What's it like? Being out on the ocean for that long?"

I sat back thinking about it. "To be honest, it's great but also hard sometimes. The ocean is a beautiful piece of water, with unknown creatures lurking below the waves. Its beautiful and frightening at the same time." I said.

"How is it frightening?" She asked me.

"Well...um...there's storms we have to be wary off, pirate ships, enemy ships, sea creatures, diseases, betrayal-" She cut me off.

"Betrayal?" She wonders her eyes interested to know more of this life on the sea.

"Yes, mutiny is always a given. Usually that happens with the crew thinks poorly of the Captain and wants off the voyage so they try to take the ship. The crew I'm traveling with is a good set of lads, so I think will be okay from that area." I seriously said.

"I see." She said.

I pointed at the lute laying next to her chair. "How long have you been using music?"

"My whole life, since I was a child. My mother was a beautiful Norwegian dancer and singer. She taught me everything I know about music, and instruments." She said as If thinking back on that time.

"You can just play the lute?" I asked Brita.

"Yes, for now but I'm trying to learn the cello." She said.

"Well, your mother taught you well." I said taking a sip of beer. "Your voice is from another world."

Brita grinned slightly. Her eyes faced mine and shown true light. "No one has ever said that about me or my voice."

"What do you mean?" I asked confused. "Your voice is beautiful and you are beautiful."

Her face blushed into violet. "Thank-thank you sir."

I nodded a smile. "But what do you mean?" I asked again.

"I usually play in taverns and Inns. I get enough money to get by, but its still not enough. Since I'm a woman, most men all they care about is having my body to themselves and sex and such. Sometimes they won't even let me play most of the time. Every man tells me the same thing, they lure me with affection and then take advantage, usually they are drunk." She frowned.

"I'm very sorry Brita. That's not right of them to do that to you." I told her keeping a stern look on my face.

"It's alright of the matter. How am I sure that your not lying to me like them? That you are complaining my complexion so you can get a piece?" She glared at me.

I put my hand across my chest as if swearing an oath. "No tricks or tomfoolery I swear of it my beautiful lady." I smiled. Brita smiled.

"Your an interesting man Henry Heartstone." She grinned.

I sat back frowning. I did enjoy the company of a good gorgeous woman in bed, but I hated seeing woman treated so poorly. It was unfair. I looked at her to see true pain in her eyes. I did the only thing I could think of. I hadn't really had many women in my life, so it was hard for me to talk or to try to be affectionate and comforting but I tried my best. I reached my hand out, setting my drink on the table. The fire still crackled in the hearth of brick. The wood creaked and fell under hot black coals and orange flurries of embers. I reached my hand out keeping it out. She looked it confused.

Another woman was now playing a guitar at this time, picking the strings and began singing Scarborough Fair, and old fashioned favorite among taverns and folklore. The woman's voice was beautiful but not as beautiful as Brita's.

"What?" She asked looking at my hand.

"Take my hand." I smiled.

"Why? What are you getting at sir?" She said sitting back.

"Just take my hand please." I grinned.

She hesitated but gripped my rough hand. She exhaled slightly from her lips. Her chest rising from breath. Her hand felt so soft and delicate and small in my rough sailor hands. My hands were rough from rigging up big rope, crates, and sword fighting.

I guided her close to the fire to where we were warm. People around the tavern were laughing and drinking loudly but I let that disturbance fade away. I just focused on the amazing lassie before my eyes. The music swirled around us.

"What is this?" She scoffed.

"Just follow my lead." I smiled.

"But I can't dance." She frowned worried.

"I'll help you my love." I smiled.

I placed one of her hands in my right hand and placed my left on her side. We swayed back and forth, stepping back and forth to the soft music that played in the background. Our feet danced and tapped on the floor boards. Her hair fell to the side of her face, the ember glow casting a golden fiery shadow on her face making her features angel like. Her eyes stared into mine with a feeling I couldn't understand but for some reason I didn't look away. We paced in circles, and she let go from my grasp halfway, and I twirled her around swinging her arm above my head, and bringing her back even closer to me. We were so close I could feel her heartbeat, beating at a rapid speed against my chest.

Brita smiled widely. We continued to dance slowly, close together.

"I've never had a man ask me to dance before." She said, I could see tears starting to form on her eyelids.

"Never?" I asked.

"Never." She frowned a tear streaming down her cheek.

I placed my finger wiping it away. I flick the wet tear into the fire. Her skin was so smooth like silk. Slowly, we got closer our eyes meeting. I closed my eyes feelingly heart thump loudly in my chest and ears. We pressed our lips together. Our lips curled onto each others, her pink lips onto mine. The music began to faded slowly, and we kissed for a good time. Finally, we pulled away and she met my eyes with a smile and then kissed me again. "Thank you for that Sir Henry." She smiled truly.

"It was my pleasure." I smiled back.

Brita bit her lip quietly and then quickly rushed to grab her lute. She picked it up and grabbed my hand and started to pull me out of the tavern. She had a look of child like wonder on her face, a happy girl truly.

"Where are you taking me?" I laughed as I pushed past people drinking in the tavern.

"Just follow me Henry." She quickly said happily as we bursted through the tavern into the cold.

I gazed through the cold air at the ship docked in the bay. The frost was forming just under the wooden hull. The air nipped at my face bitterly making me pull my scarf closer around my neck. The snow flurries rained down from the dark grey clouds from above. I took one last look at the docked ship, knowing Captain Samuel was away in his quarters looking at the manuals. I was unsure why he needed such a particular set of journals, but then again, he was captain and some captains are picky.

I looked away from the ship to see Brita looking at me, and then followed her eyes as she stopped at the ship.

"Is that the ship your on?" She pointed through the blowing snow.

I nodded. "Yes, that's the ship. Her name is Deltarone. Me, plus another 130 souls are on there besides the Captain."

"My god, that's a lot of crew members for one ship." She said in awe.

I laughed a little. "It's bigger than you think."

Brita then looked away and peered further down the snowy cobble further into the town. She then looked back at me and ushered me to follow. "Where are you taking me Brita?" I asked wondering.

She took my hand which was now purple and numb from the cold. Mine was too. "I'm taking you to my home. Come." She smiled.

I smirked to myself knowing what might become of this evening. I took her hand tightly as she guided me through twists and turns around the city. We passed by many wooden buildings, taverns, Inns, shops, houses, gardens, town squares, fountains, all under blankets of snow. I was sure this place was gorgeous in the spring time. I would have to visit it at a time, if I survive this damn voyage. The snow crunched under our boots as we continued through the cold air. The snow had covered the entire town. As we walked fast, trying to get out of the cold to get warm, we walked by a few questionable occupants of the town. A few men looked uneasy, looking at me at an angle that I disliked. I slowly put my hand on my sword that was at my right side under my coat cloak. I remembered that I had a pistol full of ball and powder with me in my pants strapped down and a cutlass at my side. If I were to encounter any unwanted visitors, I knew what to do. I gazed behind me to see our foot prints were obviously visible in the snow. After going through narrow streets, we walked up a flight of cobble stairs and took a right into a open square with houses all around. She took me to one of them on the right. We got closer to the house. It was hard to see what the house looked like from the outside because of the snow, but I could tell is was made from brown stones and burgundy wood beams just under the peeks of the snow holes, from falling snow off the roof. She pushed open a small wooden gate, knocking up the latch and closing it behind us. We walked down a path and pushed through the wooden door. Once we entered my body immediately went from cold to warm which stung my skin a little as the temperature was going back to normal.

I peered around the house as Brita took off her coat revealing a beautiful outfit.

Her noble dress flows from top to bottom and has a semi-sweetheart neckline, which lightly reveals the graceful dress worn below it. The exquisite, tightly tied fabric of her dress covers her stomach where the continuous flow is broken up by a large leather belt worn low around her waist.

Below the leather belt the dress flows down wide and hides the dress below. The front of the top dress easily reaches the ground in the front, the back continues to flow a fair length behind her and ends in a narrow rectangle.

Her sleeves are a little short and quite wide, their flow is broken up just below the

shoulder where they change color and where they're divided by simple, modest bands, these are the same fabric and color used to outline the bottom of the dress.

I grinned at her beauty. I then gazed around this house as I took off my coat and scarf hanging them on a rack near the door.

The house is equipped with a huge kitchen and two bathrooms, it also has a snug living room, three bedrooms, a cozy dining area, a playroom and a modest storage room.

I noticed that it was a nice house for someone who earned money by playing music.

66

"Quite a luxurious place?" I questioned.

Brita walked over and got a fire going in the fireplace. The fire crackled to life with orange flame.

"It was my fathers. He gave it to me before he passed." She said. She gestured me to sit next to the fire with her.

I walked over to the fire, kicking the snow off my boots. I slipped them off and dropped on the floor sitting next to her next to the warmth. We sat there, just enjoying the fire.

"Why did you bring me here?" I asked.

"Well, your the first man that has ever shown me respect so far. I figured you know, if you continued to show me respect, we could..." she trailed off standing up. I looked up at her as she began to unwove her shirt. It dropped revealing poking out breasts that were big and bold.

I gulped feeling myself getting excited. She slowly walked back a little, slowly crossing her legs, as if she was a panther lurking in the grass.

"Won't you come to bed with me?" Her Norwegian accent broke out.

"I uh....yes." I muttered.

She reached her hand out to me and I took it. She pulled me up from the floor. We slowly walked to the bedroom and she threw me back onto the comfy blue sheets. I slipped off my shirt. She climbed on top of me and smiled and kissed me passionately. We continued to kiss, and she began to sit on top. The moonlight shown through the window revealing a gorgeous glowing silver light among her naked body and we commenced to make love.

That following morning I awoke in the sunlight through the grey clouds that shone though the clear glass pane. The sun hit my face with warmth and gold, and I slowly raised up from the white pillow. The blue sheets was covering my body and I realized I was bare naked underneath. I looked to my left to see

Brita, her bare back facing me, her naked body tucked under the covers. I smiled at her, and bent over and quietly kissed her cheek. I popped my knuckles and stretched stepping out of bed. I walked over to the window and gazed down upon the wooden houses in the snow and then to the ships in the frozen bay. The snow had let up a little bit overnight, but the snow flurries still fell. I looked over at my clothes bundled up on the floor. I picked them up and slipped them on, tightening my boot buckles to keep my boots tight on my feet. As I did this Brita yawned awaking from her slumber.

I smirked a little as she sat up. She stretched her arms into the air and turned to face me.

"Hi." She smiled.

"Hey." I grinned walking over to the bed.

I squatted down to her level and kissed her. She pulled away and laid her head on the pillow softly.

"I'm still sleepy." She laughed. "Stay with me my Henry." She begged reaching her arm out to me.

"I can only for a time, but I have to head back to the Inn to retreat to Samuel for supplies to deliver. I will be able to see you later this evening though." I smiled.

"That's perfect my love." Brita smiled kissing me once again.

"I can meet you at the tavern this evening after a briefing from the captain." I smiled.

"Lovely." She smiled.

I stayed with Brita for a couple hours before heading back into the cold morning air. As I cut through the cobble streets, the snow falling, I smiled to myself under my scarf. I had gotten a women in bed, and I was in love with her and she with me. My heart thumped loudly in my chest thinking of her face inside my mind. I couldn't help but smile so widely to myself, the widest grin a man could ever grin. She was my angel.

I made it to the Inn. As I entered the room, Daniel and Tim were just leaving.

"Daniel? Tim? Where are you off too?" I wondered.

"Come Henry, the Captain needs our attendance." Tim said.

"Yes my lad, more supplies came in to deliver to the Duke of Norway."
Daniel added.

I followed them down the stairs and back out into the snow. As were trudged through the snow to the ocean bay, the ship docked tightly, Daniel looked at me.

"Where were you last night?" He asked me.

"Aye, we were getting a bit worried that the lassie lied to ya." Tim wondered.

"With Brita." I grinned looking at them both.

Tim and Daniel exchanged looks between each other, and it took them a mere minute to understand what I was saying. Then a grin formed on both of their faces.

"Henry my lad!" Daniel laughed wrapping his arm around me and Tim.

"Henry you got her in bed?" Tim smiled to me.

I nodded.

"Henry Heartstone got himself a women!" Daniel yelled through the snowy streets as it echoed down to the harbor.

"How was it?" Tim asked.

"It was good." I smiled.

Tim and Daniel looked back at each other and then Daniel nudged my shoulder a little hard.

"Can you believe this lassie? Where is the information here?" Daniel laughed.

"Tell us what happened." Tim begged.

I looked at them both clearly wanting to know what it was like. Daniel has had many women in his comfort but not in awhile and Tim not once.

"I'm not going to tell you how it happened in the bedroom." I laughed.

"What? Why not avail this?" Daniel wondered.

"It's private." I smirked.

"I've never had a woman before." Tim nervously said.

Daniel put his arm around him. "Well me lad, after we deliver this supplies, will take you to one of those whorehouses." Tim just smiled widely.

They rolled their eyes. We continued to walk in silence until we hit the harbor. We all gathered up next to the ship shielding our face from the cold wind. Within twenty minutes the whole crew was their and Captain Samuel stood higher on the dock with a load of crates stacked behind him filled with food and various weaponry. He stroked his beard slightly, and some snow flurries fell from his hair. His black cap sat on top of his head but it looked more white from the snow.

"Lads, we have gotten a new shipment. Various spices, fruits, iron, brass, ball, and the such. Now I know, you are enjoying your time here, and we have still quite awhile here, with Christmas around the corner, but we need to get these to the Duke." He nodded.

The crewmates nodded and we carried the supplies through the winter cold up to the rich temple. We dropped the crates off and the Duke was pleased with such a delivery.

After the delivery we took Tim further into the town of Bigur. We arrived at one of the whore houses. I patted his back and knocked on the iron door. A few seconds later, I heard the pitter patter of footsteps on carpet, jog up and creak open the door. It was a older woman with huge breasts annoyingly out. Her skin was wrinkly and her eyes sunken and dead. Her gray hair was in tangles. She looked at us three.

"What you want? More fuckery?" She cackled in a raspy voice.

"Um, no madam. My good friend Tim here, has never had a woman before. We want him to experience it." I smiled.

She looked Tim up and down and grinned.

"A strong built young man. Very nice. Will pair him with one of the younger girls." The older woman smiled. "Come young man."

Tim looked at us both. He looked very nervous and timid. I placed my hand on his shoulder.

"You'll be fine. You got this young man." Daniel smiled.

I gave him a nodding smile. He nodded back and he disappeared into the house. Once the door shut I looked at Daniel.

"You'll think the young lad will do well?" I asked.

"Aye, He'll be fine." Daniel laughed. "Come on, let's go get a drink at the tavern Henry."

Christmas came on fast. For Christmas, the town was lit up with lanterns and Christmas tree's with tiny red bulbs lined the windows of houses. I had gotten Brita a beautiful instrument known as the piano and she loved it. She had gotten me a new pistol, brandished clean and fast with musket ball and reloading time.

We spent Christmas, me, Brita, Daniel, and Tim together eating lovely meals of chicken and vegetables and drinking wine and ale.

Now, New Years was coming up. I knew I would be leaving soon after New Years, and Brita knew too, so we tried to spend time with each other as much as we could.

On the day of New years, me and her sat at the edge of a cobble stone wall, hanging our legs letting them dangle off the edge. We were looking at the ships docked in the cold water. On this day it was not snowing but the snow still laid flat on the ground and it was still bitter outside.

Brita held her lute next to her as we gazed at the giant wooden ships with white sails docked.

"What is that part called?" She pointed to the tall wooden stocks with the white sails.

"Oh that? That's called the main mast." I told her.

"And what's that on top? It looks like a circular gate of some sort?" She wondered.

"That's the crows nest. We usually send someone up there to spot any enemy ships with a telescope." I said.

"Well, what about that?" She asked swaying her hand across the entire deck.

"That?" I laughed loudly which startled her. "A deck. That's the main deck. On the front part of the bow, is the bow deck. Further back is the poop deck. Underneath we have barracks where we sleep, plus cannons are strapped down and muskets in the hold. There's also the Captains Cabin and quarters and then the sailors quarters under the ship." I told her.

Her eyes sparkled at the fact. "My god, that's amazing. Do you get sick sleeping?" She asked.

"Sick sleeping?" I asked confused.

"The boat constantly swaying." She noted.

"Oh, some men do but I don't. I find it calming." I smiled.

"Well what was your job on the ship?" She asked me.

"I just batted down the hatches and made sure the ship was clean and scrubbed. Check the cannons. Now, after traveling for a few months, me, my crew mates Daniel and Tim are one of the closest men that Captain trusts now." I smiled

Captain Samuel has trusted me, Daniel, and Tim more and more over the course of these months due to helping him gather the most supplies and keep order of the logs and shipments properly. Some of the other sailors had been slacking.

She nodded. I gazed at her instrument, the lute. "How do you play that thing? What are the strings called again?" I asked a little embarrassed. She had gone over it before but I had completely forgotten what she had told me because I couldn't really understand it.

"I taught you last night but I suppose you can't learn in one night." She laughed a little.

She slung her lute till it was facing me. "So the lute usually has 13 strings but, since this is a 8 Renaissance lute, it has 15 strings. So the strings here, are tuned for high and intermediate pitches, but for the two bottom strings it turns into a octave higher to keep it a lower sound. So the frets are made of horse hair that need replacing from time and time."

"Uh huh." I muttered still trying to follow.

"The lute's strings are arranged in courses, of two strings each, though the highest-pitched course usually consists of only a single string, called the chanterelle. The courses are numbered sequentially, counting from the highest pitched, so that the chanterelle is the first course, the next pair of strings is the second course." Brita smiled at me.

"I see. So, what about the bridge of the instrument?" I pointed to the bent top.

"The bridge, sometimes made of a fruitwood, is attached to the soundboard typically between a fifth and a seventh of the belly length. It does not have a separate saddle but has holes bored into it to which the strings attach directly. The bridge is made so that it tapers in height and length, with the small end holding the trebles and the higher and wider end carrying the basses. Bridges are often colored black with carbon black in a binder, often shellac and often have inscribed decoration. The scrolls or other decoration on the ends of lute bridges are integral to the bridge," Brita continued.

I blinked twice. "My god, that is quite a lot. How do you even comprehend, let alone keep ahold of such things."

"I love music and always will. It's in my blood." She smiled.

"Your right about the blood. You play amazingly." I smiled.

She grinned and kissed me.

"Now, I want you to play it." She said gesturing the lute to me.

"What?" I asked. "I can't possibly-"

"Play it my love. I'll help you." She smiled.

She handed me the lute. I slowly took it and held it sideways. It felt so light and weightless in my hands.

"Now, put your hand on the strings." She said.

I placed my left hand on the string and right hand on the neck.

"Now strum it." Brita grinned at me.

I pressed my hands on the strings and strummed it hearing a uncanny sound. It echoed through the harbor.

"Good, now the two strings on the bottom are G and H strings, the two top are A and B, grip those." She said.

I did as she told griping the four strings and strumming hearing a better sound. I grinned at her.

"See? Easy?" She laughed.

I handed her back the lute. "Easy you think?" I laughed.

"Do you know the song Watertight?" She asked me.

73

I shook my head yes. Brita began strumming the lute to the song. "Sing it with me."

"Sing it with you?" I asked.

"Please my love." She begged.

I nodded as she strummed the lute tightly. The chords bounced off the wall with such joy. She started out singing the first few lyrics, hitting the frets on point. I smiled at her as she sang with such grace. It wasn't a particularly long song, maybe around 2 minutes but it was a beautiful song. Her voice vibrated through the waters hitting against the ships making them groan to the music. After the first few notes, I joined in on the chorus. As I sang, my deep voice added perfectly to the baritone, and our voices connected together surpassingly well. She strummed the instrument faster now after the first chorus. I smiled widely and continue to sing louder getting more into the song, singing under my breath to the regular lyrics and when coming to the chorus I sang louder over the cold air. Our breath could be seen from our lips, as if it was clear dust.

The lute created a golden sound making the music seemed magical and light. Our voices, female and male, angelic and deep, baritone and soft, swirled against each other, forming under invisible notes, creating one of the most beautiful songs I could ever hear. I was so surprised with my voice that it sounded well and hearty. I wasn't bad at singing.

Brita looked at me with such love and passion. Finally, we finished the song and stared into each others eyes, not believing what just happened.

She leaned in and kissed my cold lips defrosting them with her warmth. I looked into her eyes and pulled away placing my hand on hers.

"I'm going to miss you so much my Henry." She smiled through tears.

"I'm going to miss you too my Brita." I smiled giving her one last kiss.

The next morning, we were all docking and boarding the Deltarone, ready to set sail for Dublin. I stood at the docks, holding Brita's hand tightly. Daniel brushed past me with Tim.

"Come on lad, I know your missing your lassie but we need to get a move on in these waters." He said walking up the docks with a crate.

"Pleasure to meet you madam." Tim topped off his hat to Brita.

"You as well master Timothy." Brita smiled.

I looked into her eyes as tears ran down her cheeks creating small waterfalls. I wiped them away and embraced her into a hug. I then pressed my lips to her cheek, and then her lips for a minute. I pulled away, still holding her hand.

"I will be back in Norway in due time. Soon, I promise, as fast as I can my love." I said trying to hold back sadness.

"Promise me?" She looked into my eyes with her emerald eyes.

"I promise my lady." I smiled.

"Henry, aboard!" I heard the captain yell behind me.

"I have to set sail. I promise I'll be back for you my love. It may be months, years, but my love for you will stay true and full. Only for you." I told her keeping her close.

"And mine true and full for my sailor. Be safe Henry." She muttered softly into my ear.

"Always my love." I whispered back.

"I will wait for you under candle light." She smiled.

"Good Brita. Good. I will be back." I smiled.

Brita quickly handed me a piece of paper folded up safely. I was about to unroll it to see, but she held my hand to keep me from unrolling it.

"Not now. Please, only read it when the time is right." She muttered to me.

"How will I know when the time is right?" I asked her.

"You will know. Our hearts will alined with the stars my love. You will know when the time is right." She smiled. "Keep an eye on the North Star when its brightest."

I nodded and stuffed it into my pocket. I heard the sailors above me get to work, the sails being released from the rigging. I kissed her one last time and began trotting up the wooden dock.

"I love you my sailor!" She cried to me over the cold snowy wind.

I stopped, and turned back to her. "And I love you my sweet singer." I called over the wind. I saw her eyes twinkle in the snowy air.

I smiled and trotted, hopping over the rim of the ship and my boots planting onto the dock. Daniel handed me a crate right away.

"Ah, Henry my boy, be careful with that women. Your feelings can guide you astray." He said.

I looked back at Brita waving from the bottom of the docks. I gave her a kiss goodbye as the anchor gave way and we began to churn into open waters away from Bigur, Norway. My heart stung leaving my lassie, but I knew I would come back. I will, no matter how long it takes, I will come back for her. Tim trotted over next to me, pulling out a sword and cutting the ropes tied to the poles on the side of the ship. The lower sail let way.

"Feelings aren't stray Dan. My feelings are full of love." I smiled.

"Oh lad, a women is great. Body and whatnot, feeding a man's pleasure until his penis plops off, but, watch with a watchful eye." Daniel laughed.

"Will do." I smiled.

"Aye Henry, those bitches in the whore houses, be tricky and slick. I trust no women anymore." Tim pouted.

"What? Cause a women wouldn't lick your cock? Ever think she has thoughts and feelings as well?" I asked.

"Not at all." Tim muttered.

I laughed patting his back. "You've got a lot to learn my lad."

I set the crate down on the wooden deck, gazing up at the white sails catching the cold air, pushing us further into cold waters, closer to Dublin.

March, 1679
Dublin, Ireland

Dublin was such a green country full of highlands of towering lime mountains and grey spikes and boulders that lined the fields. We had been sailing since January through the waters of cold. Finally, once March broke out and spring fell into our hands. The sky was bright baby blue with puffy white clouds hanging in the air, and the golden sun shined down upon us as we sailed into port to Dublin.

The green hills were the greenest of anything I had ever seen. I leaned over the rim of the ship, gazing out on the town. Many wooden houses and brick and stone houses dotted the cobbled streets. The cobbled streets were bustling with carriages pounding along, and the clutter clatter of horse hooves as the black vehicles trotted down the alleyways.

Many buildings looked lit up with lanterns and candles. People at the dock are loading on supplies on a few smaller ships, not as big as the Deltarone. Many men were lining the docks as the waves crashed up on the seawall behind them. The ocean water swirled and churned underneath the creaking ship as we got closer.

Captain Samuel steered the ship turning the wheel clockwise to the right and turned into port. Daniel smiled as we got closer.

"After a few months of winter, we get the warm delight of spring. More ale, and Dublin is known for it." He grinned with yellow tobacco chewed teeth.

I laughed at his remark slipping in some chew under my bottom lip and chewed on it. The tobacco sat under my gums, and I gnawed at it ever now and then tasting the salt. I spit on the deck, my salvia a swirl of clear and red. "I'm pleased to be tasting the ale here." I laughed as the boat got closer to the dock.

Tim threw a stone into the ocean, the stone splashing into the water creating a funneled water spray. "I love ale lads." He laughed.

"Don't we all laddie?" Daniel croaked with a wide toothed grin.

"Hehe, Tim, you so crazy, asking such a question like that." I spat.

The ship docked and we unloaded some supplies and headed down to the dock. We carried the supplies through the town. The town was magical. Taverns sat on every corner, houses of wood and brick, chimneys smoking high, and the smell of sizzling meats and sweets filled my nostrils. People were walking up and down the streets, men, women, and children dancing, laughing, drinking, eating, playing music, fucking. Whorehouses sat on the left side of the road, along with bakeries, blacksmiths, horse stables, churches, and such more. As we continued down the street, a fight was broken out. A few men surrounded two young gents swinging punches at each others faces. Blood was laid a little on the cobble from their blows. The men cheered and ranted throwing money on the young lads. A little further down older gents were twiddling fiddles and banjos singing and strumming. People around them danced some hearty rigs and jigs. Moss was forming and gorowing between the cracks of the street. The whole city of Dublin was filled with light and magic, as if it was alive itself.

As we jogged through the town, knowing drink will treat us later on, we came to a stop near a town square. The town square wasn't occupied. Buildings lay about, and the fat highland grey mountains echoed in the background of the land. I peered behind me to see the ships only dots in the bay, for we had jogged a few miles with heavy wooden boxes. The people were laughing and drinking and enjoying themselves further deeper into the city, and I could hear the Irish accent being slurred. A fountain of women sat in front of us. Naked women made of stone, spouted water from their mouths into the water at the bottom of the stone bowl, their bodies laying on one another erotically. We stacked the crates on one another, the various supplies categorized together. Samuel rested on the fountain rim clasping his hands together. He looked much older, his eyes sunken in, his skin more aged.

"Take rest lads." He said. "We are waiting for the man we give the supplies too."

The crew sighed for rest and laid against the buildings and all around the square. Samuel called us three over. Me, Daniel, and Tim. We walked over and sat near him.

"Sir?" I asked him.

"Young lads, I was thinking to myself the other night. The man we are meeting, a Earl of Ireland, knows the German waters more than anyone. For me, not the much. Daniel you know the German waters aye?" Samuel asked him.

Daniel smiled. "Aye sir. I know those waters well enough. I can help guide ya through to avoid any enemy ships."

"Perfect." Samuel smiled dryly.

"Sir, who is this Earl?" Tim asked.

"This Earl his name is Colin Baggins. A mighty sailor along the German and Irish sea's. He's fought many battles, won many, but had betrayed many of his own for gold and silver. He's a sleek one, I'll tell you that much, but a good man no doubt." Samuel croaked.

"If he is sleek should we keep an eye on the man?" I asked curiously.

"Aye, just in case, we should keep an eye watchful." Samuel nodded.

"You can trust us sir." I smiled.

Samuel clasped my shoulder. "I trust you three lads and you three only. Now, let's get this done and go have a lovely drink of cold ale."

I smiled at the old man. I had become fond of our captain. He was a good sailor and navigator, and he trusted me and my best friends. He had a good heart and a stern backside for work and sailing and knew his waters well.

A short time later, I heard the clap of hooves echo down to my ears. I looked up from the fountain and saw a black horse stopping and hauling a few feet to my left. The black horse was big and powerful. As it breathed through its nostrils its belly extended in and out. Its crystal blue eyes gazed at everyone trying to decide what was happening at this moment in time. His black mane lined down the back of its neck and draped over the side, and its sharp ears perked up listening to the sounds around of people bustling about.

It stone hooves clamped the ground in place and its stringy tail swayed side to side as it sniffed and puffed out noises from its pouty fat lips. Its hips were bold and big, and I could see the muscles and tendons working beneath the flesh of the black fur. Sitting on top of the beast, was a burly man. He slid off his boots smacking the stone loudly and made a clink sound as he approached the Captain. His arms were ripped, blue veins throbbed on the outer edges of his hairy arms. His hands were massive and boney. He wore a green teal shirt and under that held up buy a belt was a plaid kilt and below that was socks and boots. He had a steaming wooden pipe in his fat lips. His nose was big and poked out like a bird beak. He grinned at the Captain with yellow grainy teeth. His red hair on top of his head was curly, and he had a big bushy red beard across his face, that took up under his nose with a mustache that curled under at the ends. His eyes were as green as the Irish Hills behind me.

As he got into face to face distance with Samuel they stared at each other for a time, not speaking and the whole crew was silent. Even the guards that flanked Colin were still with muskets and their green jackets. Then Colin Baggins coughed out a wheezy laugh and clasped Samuel in a hug who then smiled too.

"Samuel! How are you?" He spoke with such an intense Irish accent, that I couldn't be sure if his accent was Irish or English. It was so distinct that you could pick it out almost immediately.

"I'm well, thank you and you?" Samuel smiled.

"As good as a women's organismic feeling!" He laughed loudly and some of the crew laughed with him.

"Great to hear Colin." Samuel clapped his shoulder hard with such joy. "Where have you been as of late?"

The burly man sat down on the fountain rim resting himself. The entire crew looked at the man with intrigue.

"I've been all over my friend. Recently I just sailed into port a month ago from Italy. I was visiting Rome, specular city with beautiful belly dancers, exquisite foods, and building of colossal sizes." Baggins raised his arms in a circle formation to show how big it was, or bigger.

"My god." Samuel's eyes sparkled.

"Indeed. Now, I just sailed back to Dublin to rest my legs and give my crew a break, we had been out at sea for a few years, jumping around from the Caribbean, to Brazil, to India, to Africa." He continued.

"Where is your crew now? I don't see them with you, not one soul." Samuel said looking around in a raspy voice.

"Aye, there enjoying themselves in the town. You may see them later, most likely in the taverns. How long are you staying for Samuel?" Colin asked.

"A week or so. Once we leave here, we are on the course towards Germany." Samuel said.

"Germany? What's there?" He asked abruptly.

"Just like what we are doing here, dropping off some supplies, even though we are seeing amazing places for short times, this voyage is a simple drop and run." Samuel said.

"Oh laddie, I remember those, pain in the arse I'd say. Why are you taking supplies to these people?" He wondered.

"London just went through a devastating fire a decade back, so we deliver, they provide gold and silver, which in turn helps London flourish again to its common wealth as it once was." Samuel said.

"Aye, I heard of the fire, when was it again?" Colin asked.

"1666, the great fire of London, and soon after the Black Plague struck us, taking the lives of millions. We are still recovering." Samuel frowned at the thought.

I remembered the Great fire of London. I was 13 or 14 when it had happened. No one truly knows how it started, but it took and burned almost half the city to ash and coal. Millions burned alive under the flames and crashing bell towers and castles. The golden city of London was a fiery red Hellish landscape after it was put out. All I could recall from it was my father and mother had taken me and my younger sister, out to the country side. We had gotten out by carriage and lived with our Aunt Margot for a month or so in

81

the farm lands. Once the fire was done, and the crisp bodies were fetched out of burning houses and streets, we moved back to see our house was destroyed. Not a speck of wood left. Over time, we built a new house a few blocks down from our older one, and then soon the Black Plague shot out when I was eighteen years of age. Dark times, just dark times, I shivered to myself thinking back on that horrid time, it was as if the Devil walked the earth. I looked back at the two captains.

"My god, Samuel, I'm sorry. Well, I'm glad London is getting back on its feet." Colin smiled.

"Thank you, me as well. So, encounter any battles on your trips?" Samuel asked.

"Aye. Some nasty ones. Three months ago, my ship had a run in with one of those French ships. Damn fucking bastards, burn the hull of my girl, to a black tar, but we blew them under the waves soon enough. Lost a lot of good men sadly, but what's a captain gonna do?" He laughed.

Samuel kept a stern look. I could drastically tell that Colin didn't really care about his crew as much as Samuel did. I think that's what separated them a bit.

"Anyway, I'm sorry about your ship, is it still burnt?" Samuel asked.

"No, no, got her fixed up a couple weeks ago. Now, she's shiny and new as ever." Baggins smiled happily. His red bush jiggled as he smiled.

"I heard some time ago, a few years in fact, you were teaching up in Cork, Ireland at the college, what for?" Samuel asked.

"Yes lad, I was magister for a year or two up in Cork, teaching philosophy, but that life got too dull and I missed the ocean. I needed her under my wing again." Baggins said.

"I see. Can't really see you as a magister Colin." Samuel croaked.

"Aye, wasn't the right fit." He said more seriously.

There was a moment of silence between them and then Colin puckered out his fat lips under his red mustache. His plaid kilt swayed as he stood up from the fountain.

"How about those shipments lad?" He smiled standing above Samuel.

"Of course." Samuel gritted his teeth.

I could tell something wasn't right between them, like they had some nasty history together, maybe it was because Captain Samuel was stuck with supply duty still. Samuel nodded to me and Daniel and Tim. We three headed over and popped off the tops of the crates. Colin pranced around, examining the contents that lay in each box, eyeing the supplies carefully.

"Everything is there Colin." Samuel said.

"I believe you. Just double checking." Baggins smirked.

Colin paced through the crates and then nodded to himself. "Everything seems to be in order."

Within a few minutes Samuel received the coin and shook hands with the Irishman. They talked for a few minutes and then Colin laughed loudly.

"How about we get a drink at the tavern?" He asked Samuel and Samuel obliged.

Colin had the crates hurried off and we trotted down through the town, until we hit a tavern before us. This tavern was amazing and bigger than the one in Norway. It was made of birch wood with black stained glass windows on the sides and a upstairs. Entering through the doors, it was packed with men and woman of race. Irish, Swedish, Scottish, Belgium and more. Men were drinking and laughing happily as they ate good food and drank ale and rum. Women danced and sang, and ate as well, sitting atop of men's laps with their arms around them. Seeing women made me miss Brita, but I knew in my heart I would see her again.

Me, Daniel, and Tim ordered some rum and sat at a oak table near a window that looked out on the street with people walking by and carriages trotting along past.

I gripped my wooden mug and drank it throughly. The rum stung my throat and slapped my tongue with a honey taste which was yummy. Daniel sat in front of me while Tim was next to me. We drank for a minute, as I watched Samuel take a seat a few tables down from us, with Colin. Daniel spun around in his small chair gazing at the two captains bantering over drink and laughing.

"Something about Baggins gots me all uneasy." Daniel muttered lowly to me and Tim.

"What do you mean?" I asked.

"I'm not sure but he reeks of something. I can smell it, and I know when something is off." Daniel muttered.

"What is off Master Dan?" Tim asked.

Daniel eyed Tim." I told you, you don't have to call me Master Daniel, Daniel or Dan is fine." He said gulping his honey rum.

I took a sip of mine feeling the sweet honey suckle hit my taste buds. "Tell me Dan, what exactly is off?"

"That Irish lad, Colin Baggins, I've heard stories about him." Daniel grinned.

"Stories?" Tim asked.

"Aye, stories lads." Daniel smiled.

We sat there for a minute waiting for Daniel to speak and continue but he just sat there drinking his rum.

"Well?" Me and Tim both said at the same time.

"Well what?" Daniel asked.

"What stories, you just said, 'I've heard stories', and the sat there gwaking of the like." I laughed.

"Aye!" Daniel raised his mug high and yelled. He set it back down. "Stories indeed. I've heard, that ole Baggins was fighting a mighty Spanish ship. A fleet so powerful, that they had over a thousand canons on board her, and clad iron guns so thick that it was as if the the whole ship was iron. They took her on, and Colin was losing the battle, so what I heard was he burned his own ship, to get off in their rowboats so the Spanish could not get their treasure. He even burned most of his own men alive."

"You believe that?" Tim asked.

"Aye, I do. Don't you?" Daniel eyed us both.

"No." Tim said.

"Believe what you like, I don't trust him." Daniel said.

"Ah, Dan, your just paranoid. Nothing of the matter." I smiled.

Suddenly I saw the Irish Captain leave the tavern quickly. I watched him outside through the window for a minute and then he took off in a run down the street.

"Oi, look at that." I elbowed Tim and Daniel. They peered out the window at the sprinting Captain.

"Wonder what that was about?" Tim asked.

"I don't know." Daniel said.

Suddenly, then, Captain Samuel placed his hand down on the edge of our table. We all looked up at him, and he grinned widely.

"I'm going to be level with you lads." He said quietly.

"Uh, level sir?" I asked him.

"Hold on, let me grab a quick drink and I'll join you gents." He said staggering off to the counter.

I gave Dan and Tim a odd eye and they just shrugged. Samuel returned to the table with a drink and sat between Tim and Daniel. The Captain leaned in a bit closer to the table.

"Um, sir, are you alright?" Tim asked him.

"Aye young Tim, I'm alright." He said. "What's the matter?"

"Well, usually the captain doesn't sit with crew men." I said.

"Can't a captain bond with his mates?" He laughed.

"Of course." Daniel said. "But sir, we just saw Colin jog down to the bay?"

"Oh aye, yes. He's just fetching a few things from his ship. He'll be back." Samuel said. "But I'm here to let you three in on a little secret, because I trust you three lads."

"Secret sir? What secret?" I asked.

Samuel leaned back in his chair. "Aye. Now, this may sound a bit crazy but bear with me." He said.

He reached into his leather bag and pulled out a journal. The same journal Tim had described to us in Norway. Samuel placed it on the table but didn't open it. The leather bound booklet was smooth and smelled of fresh pressed leather. A small thread kept it tied shut on the front.

The Captain placed his hand on the front of it. "Lads, this voyage isn't just for delivering supplies. I am searching for something that has been a legend to man for hundreds of years. It has been mystical for the ocean for some time. Thousands of years. I have been searching for years and now I finally have a map to where they are located mostly." Samuel grinned happily.

"What thing are you referring too?" I asked.

Samuel looked around the tavern to make sure the other customers weren't listening in. He leaned in very close as we huddled up. "Mermaids."

All three of us blinked. "Mermaids sir?" Tim asked.

"Yes lads. Mermaids. The mystical sea woman that swim beneath the waves." He said.

"What about them? Daniel asked.

"That's what I'm doing. Not only am I delivering supplies to get us gold and silver, but I'm also searching for them. All of my life, I've been told stories by sailors who have claimed to have seen them, but there is no documentation to their existence. I want to find one and prove to the world that they exist, I know they do." Samuel said.

"But sir, they are not real, myths of such." Daniel said.

"That's what most people believe yes, but not me. I know they are real." He said.

"You know sir, that they are just stories." Tim said.

"Yes young lad, but to me they are maps. Maps to find where they are." He said. "Which is why..." He trailed off opening the journal to reveal detailed descriptions of mermaids and images of them drawn out. "I have this."

"What is this exactly?" I asked.

"This is Christopher Columbus journal from 1492. His journal. I bought it off a man in Norway, and it's his because of this." Samuel said flipping the journal over.

Behind the journal on the very bottom etched in the leather was his signature. All of our eyes widened in amazement.

"My god sir." I smiled widely as Dan and Tim did the same.

"Aye. There is a detailed description of this creature from him when he was off the coast of Madagascar. That's where he explained seeing a women with a fish for a tail and half body. Just off the coast of Kings Bay, in Madagascar." He smiled.

He flipped out a map and unrolled it across the table. We all three peered down at it seeing blue and red lines stringing across the paper over the drawn waves and waters and landmarks. Samuel pointed his finger at a land mass just off Madagascar.

"That is where we are going. King's bay lads. There is said to be jungles filled with creatures of such origin that no other place has them roaming. Also, it is the said place, that Columbus said he saw the mermaid." Samuel smiled happily, and he flipped through a few pages in the journal. He stopped on a drawn out image of a mermaid. The half fish and half beautiful women, had long brown hair that curled down to her naked breasts. Her orange and seaweed green tail with giant orange fins that split in two at the bottom. A record of the description recorded by Columbus himself was at the bottom of the image. I ushered the journal over and looked at it, as Samuel handed it to me. As I did this, he reached into his leather bag and pulled out another leather book.

"Henry, if this is real...we can....we could be marked down in history as miracles if we find a mermaid." Daniel smiled. "Timothy!" He laughed clapping his shoulder.

Tim's eyes widened of the glory we would receive back in England for this.

"Lads, imagine the glory and gold we will get back home for capturing and taking a mermaid home!" He smiled.

"Untold riches." Tim's mouth watered.

"Lads, do you believe me?" Samuel asked.

We all nodded in fact. I had never really believed my fathers stories about sirens but seeing this, made me believe in them now.

"Why do you need us?" Daniel asked the captain.

"I trust you lads. I need your help in finding one of this mystical creatures. If you help me, capture one, and bring it back to London, us four will split the riches." Samuel smiled. "You all in?"

"We're in." I said. "Just let me read this description of the mermaid." I said.

"Of course, take your time. I have another booklet to show as well." Samuel said.

I gazed at the passage describing what she looked like. I passed the journal to Tim who read it and then Daniel. Samuel slipped me the another journal in which I opened. There was another passage.

"That journal was Henry Hudsons. He was off near Madaagscar when he saw the mermaid. It was recorded in 1608." Samuel said.

The passage read:

"*This morning one of our company, looking overboard, saw a mermaid, and calling up some of the company to see her, one more came up, and by that time she was come close to the ship's side, looking earnestly on the men. A little while after a sea came and over- turned her. From the navel upward her back and breast were like a woman's, as they say that saw her; her body as big as one of ours; her skin very white, and long hair hanging down behind, of colour black. In her going down they saw her tail, which was like the tail of a porpoise, and speckled like a mackerel. Their names that saw her were Thomas Hilles and Robert Rayney.*"

My eyes widened. "I've heard stories of Henry Hudson through the Norwegian seas. He was a well known explorer and navigator in Norway."

"Aye, he was a good one. Sadly he passed in 1645, I wish I could ask him what he saw." Samuel frowned.

"This is amazing. I have heard many tall tales of this mythical mer-women." Tim said. "I do know that they are mostly evil correct?"

"Aye, they have the most beautiful singing voice known to man, but its a death trap. They sing to you, and lure you to your death. There voice sort of puts you in a trance, you have no control over yourself and walk to her like a mindless man. As if your mind is not your own. Then they usually talk too you sometimes, or they just kill you and drown you and eat you." Daniel noted.

Tim shivered. "God, that's horrible. Why are they such deceiving beauties?"

"I do not know there nature or the nature of why they do what they do, but we will find one and capture one." Samuels eyes danced with adventure.

We all nodded to him. Samuel handed me one last journal. "Here. This was John Smiths."

I opened it and read a recording from his. It read: "the upper part of her body perfectly resembled that of a woman, and she was swimming about with all possible grace near the shore." It had "large eyes, rather too round, a finely shaped nose (a little too short), well-formed ears, rather too long, and her long green hair imparted to her an original character by no means unattractive."

"John Smith was an English man. Even he found one near there. This maybe the breeding ground or something of these mermaids." I said.

"I know there are many shipwrecks that happened there." Daniel said.

"Why do you think their are many shipwrecks?" Samuel asked him.

"Because they sing to the sailors and lure them to crash into the rocks near the reefs." Tim shivered with fear.

"Aye lads. But us, us, we will not fall for their songs and lies. Now." Samuel slammed his mug down and then raised it high. We three raised it as well.

"Whose with me to find a mermaid lads?"

"Aye!" We cheered and drank happily.

We sat our mugs down and leaned back in our chairs full of rum and ale. Samuel flicked a few coins to the bar tender and we were brought a warm meal of meats of chicken and duck. Sizzling starches sat on the sides of our plates and we ate happily together sharing great stories of our lives. As we talked I asked Samuel a question.

"When did you purchase the Deltarone?" I asked.

"Oh lad, in 1654. She's years old and runs well under the waves." He laughed happily.

"Your right about the fast part. I'm sure she can run out any vessel." Daniel smiled eating a piece of meat.

"Correct. She's a fast one. I'm proud to wield her helm." Samuel smiled.

"What's it like being captain?" Tim asked.

Samuel sat back puzzled, like he had never been asked that question before. Tim was a young man and questioned almost everything and everybody because he didn't know better but I was actually glad he asked it.

Samuel sipped his ale. "Being Captain is a duty and responsibility. It can rewarding in the end, but also dangerous and difficult. I have to keep you men and my crew in line, make the decisions, answer most of the questions, provide, voyage, adventure and do everything." He frowned.

"Do you like it?" I asked.

"Sometimes yes but sometimes no. Its a hard life lads, and what we do is a hard life out on the sea. The sea is a mystical one, a tricky one, you never know what will happen. When I see you lads working hard but laughing it makes me think back on the time when I was still young and bold like you all. Now, I'm old." He smirked.

"Ah, well, you got a few years on us." I laughed.

We all laughed together. I took a sip of my drink and finished my meal.

"When are we setting sail?"

"A few days from now." Samuel said. "Enjoy the drink."

We all took a sip of ale and smiled. A few minutes later, I heard a man stumbling over to our table. He was a middle aged man with gray hairs forming on his brown scalp. He had scruff on his face, glassy eyes, and dirty clothes. He clearly was drunk. He stumbled by a table, toppling onto it catching himself, then slowly standing up and burping. He then turned towards us and stopped in front of our table.

"Can I help you sir?" The Captain asked.

"Aye you can help me." He bleched.

"Alright, with what?" Samuel asked him.

"Help me..." He coughed and then vomited on the side wall making it turn from stone to yellow corn and peas. He wiped his mouth, and licked off the throw up on his knuckles. I almost threw up just seeing that. He then faced the Captain.

"Help me understand this talk about mermaids." The drunk man muttered.

"I beg your pardon sir?" Samuel asked.

"You heard me. I heard ya'll speaking of siren's and such. Bad talk. Bad talk. Talking of them brings them here, and we can't have that in Dublin." The man burped.

"Sir, your drunk." Samuel said.

"No I'm not, you mother fucker." He yelled at him pulling out a dagger.

"How dare you use that tongue towards me! I am a officer and captain by English law!" Samuel yelled pulling out his pistol and cocking it aiming it at the man's head.

The whole tavern of people was in a stand still. Some people who were sitting down froze in fear while a few men behind the drunk man stood up and pulled out swords. Daniel, Tim, and I stood up, my hand on my hilt. The bar tender was frozen behind the counter.

"Do it." The drunk man spat at the captain.

Samuel cocked his pistol and put his finger on the trigger.

"Sir not here!" I yelled.

"Get the fuck out of my tavern!" The bar tender yelled.

Samuel cocked his pistol and swung it to the bar tender. "I'd be careful who your talking too!"

"Address me then." The bar tender smiled.

"Captain Samuel under the travel and protection of the English King!" He screamed through the entire tavern I was sure it hit everyones ears.

The bar tender frowned at the comment. The drunk man laughed at the captain and pointed his finger up with the middle finger. "Fuck you Sir. English men don't belong here."

The Captain gave him such angry, I thought his eyes were from Hell itself. The Captain slowly placed his finger on the black trigger. The pistol was about to let out a bullet. I grabbed Samuel's arm aiming his gun into the air. The gun popped off with a loud bang, sending the bullet thorough the roof and creating a clump of blue smoke. The drunk man stumbled back in shock after the gun went off. Everyone in the tavern gasped and sat and stood in awe and shock. Daniel then grabbed his empty plate and smashed it across the face of the drunk man. He rolled his eyes into his head and fell backwards smacking his head on the edge of the table and laid out cold.

"Don't you ever speak ill of our captain you cunt fuck!" Daniel screamed at the out cold man. Everyone just stared at us, and din't say anything.

The Captain looked at the bar keep and slowly put down his pistol. "Come on lads."

We cleaned up our things and hustled out of the tavern bursting into the humid air of Ireland. We staggered down the street. As we walked down the street through Dublin, Captain Samuel growled angrily.

"Stubborn asshole. Dublin is full of drunk men." He muttered. "Come on lads, let's head back to the Inn."

A few days passed after the tavern drunkard incident and we were ready to set sail for Germany. We didn't return to that tavern again for good reasons, and I was shocked to see Captain Samuel would take a innocent man out like that. I knew he was out of line, but regardless it was shocking. We had boarded the coin under the deck near the Captains quarters. Samuel said his goodbyes to Colin as we let the sails way, and untied the rigging to give the Deltarone some air to churn into the ocean. After they goodbyes' Samuel climbed on board his ship and took the wheel. I gazed up at the Irish highlands shining bright green in the sunshine.

"Onward gents! To Germany!" Captain Samuel bellowed over the wheel.

Part 2

Blood, Powder, and Storms

June, 1679
Off the Coast of Germany

I sat up in the crows nest with a telescope, aiming it down, and gazing across the wide ocean blue. The telescope was made of gold with a clear scope to look through. I put one eye through the glass, seeing through the slightly fogged up glass at the water in the distance.

These past months we have passed a few friendly English ships to trade supplies with and get a few more sailors, but other than that it's been nothing. We haven't seen any enemy ships which was good but also very odd. Most voyages by now, would have seen a few but us, not once. I knew we were off the coast of Germany, and I had been stationed up in the crows nest to look out for any landmasses, and incoming ships but nothing, just open endless water. The heat has been torture burning down on us giving our skin a red burn, and making our mouths run dry after working in the heat. We are running low on pure fresh water as well. As I scanned the horizon for anything, Tim called up to me from below.

"Oi, Henry! Captain Samuel needs us in his quarters, come on down!" He bellowed up from the deck.

I set the telescope down beside me and closed it up. I slipped it into my pocket and gazed down at the deck seeing the sailors running about carrying supplies and stocking canons and guns, and appearing up and down from under the ship. The rowboats sat on either side, as they were being fastened down tight with rope.

I crouched under the nest, and slipped down to the rope of webs. I hurried down placing my foot carefully on each rope square to make sure I wouldn't fall. I hurried down the rope and landed with a plop on the wooden deck. The sun shined down from the sky, creating a ungodly heat on the back of our necks and heads. Tim stood before me, his shaggy blonde hair to his shoulders and his face with a light scruff. His eyes were firmer than when we started this voyage, and his arms and torso was being built up and more muscular. My hair was tied in a bun behind my head to keep it out of my eyes. The wind howled in my ears.

"What's the Captain need?" I asked young Tim.

"Follow me below deck, he needs to talk to us." Tim ushered me to follow.

I followed young Tim deeper into the ship. I paced forward on the deck, looking to my left out on the mystical blue. The sun glared off the top of the water creating a mirror of sorts to show us our own swirly reflection. I wondered what creatures really did lurk below in the deep dark waters. I still had a few doubts of these magical mermaids, did they really exist? Have I seen one before and I mistook it for a natural sea creature because my eyes didn't want to understand it? In my heart, I hope those beauties are real and whole. I looked at the back of Tim as we descended the steps below deck hearing the creak under our boots. We went below deck passing through the barracks were empty rope hammocks, and some full of snoring sailors swung lightly in the ocean sway. Iron black canons were strapped down at either sides facing outward through holes of the ship. We took another flight of stairs further down. Below that deck were stacked crates of gold and coin, supplies of sorts, and the smell of oil stung my nose. I followed Tim, taking a swift turn to the left to a wooden door. He pushed it open and we stepped inside. Once inside Tim closed the door and locked it behind us. I saw Captain Samuel sitting at his desk, with a map rolled out before him, and Daniel standing over him pointing to some spots and talking to him. I gazed around the captains quarters. I had only been here a few times but it was nice and fancy. A teal and gold rug lay on the wood planks through out the room. A soft velvet bed sat to my right, with a few chests full of charts, maps, and documents near it. The desk was carved from aspen wood from England, and it always looked polished and new. Behind the desk was a stainless clear wide window that looked from behind the ship out on the water. To my left was a cabinet full of whiskey, rum, and beer, and a table with a white cloth and china ware and silver ware. Food was stocked under in some drawers.

"You see sir? If we continue down these routes we will cut the time in half. Traveling by this sun and star, we will be behind course." Daniel added. Captain Samuel, not looking up from his big map put his hand up as if he was interrupting Dan. His white beard shook as he spoke. "I know master Daniel, but I want to get to Kings Bay as quick as possible, to be honest I wish we could skip Germany. I don't find it important."

"The crew would question it." Daniel said.

"Aye lad, I know, I know." Samuel put his rough hand under his chin thinking.

"You don't want the crew to know?" I asked abruptly.

Both Daniel and Samuel looked up from the map. Daniel smiled slightly when he saw me and Tim. Samuel froze for a minute and then nodded.

"Yes, I don't want them to know only us. If they know, there either think I'm crazy and will try to over throw me, or want a piece of the cut. Only us four need to know about this and handle this." Samuel said. "Understand?"

"I understand." I said.

"As do I sir." Tim nodded too.

"Good. Now, Henry, how is the crows nest going? Any scouting of ships? Reports?" Samuel urgently wanted to know.

"Uh, no sir. A few friendlies, but no enemies. It's strange to say the least." I muttered.

"Aye, it's odd, I haven't seen any either." Tim said.

"None?" Daniel asked.

"None." I said.

"Shit, that's not right, we are definitely in German waters." Samuel thought leaning back propping his boots up.

"Somethings a miss I'm sure." I said.

"Tim, supply reports? Anything missing or all accounted for? How are the muskets and ball of powder? Tell me please we still have those blunders." Samuel croaked.

"Aye sir. I checked them this morning early just before the sun jumped the clouds. All supplies accounted for, grains are about 45 pounds and musket

96

ball 68 pounds of lead. Blunder busses in check and loaded and safe." Tim nodded.

"Splendid. You lads are my saviors, I'll tell you that." Samuel laughed. "Hungry?"

"A bit yes." Me and Tim said.

"Aye here." Samuel said.

He bent down and opened a small drawer from under his desk. "I usually only have these for myself but since you lads are helping me, you deserve a bite of it." He pulled out a small cigar box. He opened the box but there was no cigars in there, but mangos.

He tossed me one and I caught it. It was smooth and the red and green skin looked rough to eat. He gave one to Tim, then Daniel, and then he took one himself. He closed the box and slid it under his desk.

"Mangos. Freshly imported from India." Samuel grinned taking a bite.

I sank my teeth into the skin tearing it away and finally finding the golden flesh. The sweet suckling flesh of the fruit filled my tongue with sweet, such sweet. The golden meat of the fruit was so juicy and ripe I kept eating it.

"So..." Samuel burped through his mango. "We are just off the coast of Germany, we should reach it by tomorrow. After Germany we head through Africa, towards Madagascar. That's where we can start looking for the mermaid."

I walked over and plopped into one of his wooden desk chairs as did Tim. I took a bite of the mango and propped my boots up on the table. Daniel leaned against the glass behind Samuel.

"What about the crew?" I asked.

"The rest of the crew will wonder why we are aimlessly searching through the jungle." Tim brought up.

Samuel thought stroking his beard. "That's a problem."

"A big problem, unless you'd offer them a cut but I know you don't want to..." I Trailed off.

"Aye, no cut, I don't want to deal with that hassle. Will figure out a solution once we get to that point." Samuel said. "For now, let's focus on getting to King's Bay in one piece."

Suddenly a explosion sounded from above deck. The whole ship shook violently. I toppled out of the chair dropping the fruit. Daniel stumbled to the ground.

"Bloody hell! What the hell was that?" Samuel croaked.

I regained my balanced and pulled Tim up. Another sounded, this time a canon ball of black tearing through the wood to my right. I ducked hitting the ground and taking Tim with me, as wood split and flew above our heads.

"We are under attack!" I shouted. "To above deck!"

I jumped up and we all rushed up the stairs. As I ran through the second below deck, I picked up a musket and cutlass. I strapped the sword to my right side under my belt, as I grabbed a handful of musket iron lead ball, and shoved them in my pocket. I grabbed a horn of black powder and slung the leather strap across my chest. Daniel and Tim did the same, except Daniel grabbed a blunder buss. Samuel pushed past us and we trotted up the deck into the sunlight. Once we broke light, the whole crew was running around, screaming, and uniting the canons. They threw the ropes off the iron giants, and began pushing them towards the right. I looked up over the rim to see a giant wooden ship with red sails facing right to us. A crew on their side were doing the same, except they were reloading their canons for another blow. The red sails had skulls on the front of the cloth. I could see the captain standing by the wheel, staring us down, but he was too far away to see what he looked like. Our crew began grabbing big iron canon balls as some of the iron balls rolled across the deck as people ran along, arming themselves with muskets and daggers.

"It's a damn German ship! Lads give them hell! Will sink her down to the depths!"

Samuel screamed to his mighty crew and we all yelled with no fear.

To be honest, I was so scared, and I didn't want to die but I had sailing with this bunch of lads for almost a year. I was willing to go down fighting with them, or go down with the ship with my two best mates. I saw the other men aim the canons towards us. The lit the fuse and it sizzled down the iron beasts. They exploded and a cloud of white and grey smoke escaped the barrel. The balls sped towards our ship. A few hit under the hull blowing holes into the ship. A few others sailed over our heads, missing us. They reloaded within a minute, and by now we had gotten the canons pushed forward aiming at their ship.

They fired another round at us. The canon balls pierced the mast this time.

"Duck!" I yelled as a ball sped towards us.

I hit the deck dropping my musket by my side. Tim and Daniel and half the other of the crew hit the ground as the canon ball smashed into the left side of our canons. Our canons popped up into the air, rolling onto the other canons, and breaking in half, and exploded into a orange flame. A couples canons flipped over and landed on a few crew mean squishing them to pancakes while some perished in the fire, while some others flew over board. They fired another round splitting the wood up making some of the rim of the boat peel off and plop into the ocean. They hit more of our canons on the left side, making them roll down the deck and smash into the stairs up to the wheel deck snapping some of the edges off. Crew men rolled around on the deck, dropping canon balls and bullets. An orange fire escaped and scattered across the left side of the deck and I watched a few men try to dump water on it to put it out. A canon ball flew taking off the head clean off on one of the sailors. Two of the canons exploded sensing me flying back, smacking my head on the back of the wood of the ship. My head throbbed and my ears rang to the sound of muffled voices. Daniel crawled over to me as I saw Tim loading his musket. Daniel picked me up and slapped my face hard.

"Come on lad! Get up! We need to fire these iron!" He screamed at me.

I nodded and stood up running over to the canons on the right side. I clasped onto one as me and Daniel shoved it towards the ship. Tim tossed me a rod with oil on the tip. I lit the fuse and the fuse on the back of the iron sped and clipped away. Soon the canon fired a ball, a flume of smoke escaped the hole, and the ball smashed into the front side of the ship sending a few canons and men back in a fire of orange and red blood.

The rest of our crew began lining the canons and lighting the fuses quickly. The canons rang off one by one at the ship, blowing holes in the wood, sending men flying. The balls of iron destroyed into the ship sending the sailors into the sea. They struggled to swim.

"Shoot them lads!" Cried Samuel.

I quickly equipped my musket, and picked up a musket ball. I shoved it down the muzzle, then grabbed the rod which was attached to the front of the weapon. I slammed the rod into the muzzle shoving the bullet further down in the shaft of the gun. I pulled the rod out once the bullet was snug, and placed it back in place. I then opened my powder cask and poured in the black grains hearing it think down the barrel. I then flipped my gun clasping it forward, and lit a match against them wood of the planks. I lit the fuse as it sizzled orange, I cocked the gun back and aimed down the sight at the swimming away sailors to the fiery ship. Canons still rang out from either ships as both our ships exploded into a orange, as wood flew up into the sky. The sails were being shot through, holes as big as craters forming.

The ships creaked and groaned, and the pop and bang of musket fire echoed in my ears. I aimed my sights down at the drowning sailors trying to swim to the safety of the ship. Some of the other sailors on my side, had been firing, creating water sprays missing the sailors on purpose. I aimed down the sight at a sailor and fired. The musket ball shot through the air, and split the sailors skull in two and he dropped dead floating softly in the waves. The blue turned a dark red. I quickly reloaded and fired again hitting a man in the arm making him scream in pain and he sank beneath the water since he couldn't use his arms to keep himself afloat. Tim fired his gun next to me, putting the butt of it to his right shoulder. He fired the gun, the muzzle stinging a white smoke, and the bullet piercing a man's flesh just under the head in the side of the neck. His neck popped open and pieces of bones flew out of his flesh. Tim turned to me and I smiled back at him.

Canon balls rang towards us, and we ducked under the rim of the ship as the balls hit our mast. The mast creaked and groaned but stayed put. I peered over the side of the ship to see the crew on the German side, they were struggling to reload their guns. They Popped off a few shots, and I could hear and feel the vibration of the bullets hitting the wood near us or the zip over our heads, but they were struggling and falling fast.

A few bullets hit some of our sailors who were hit in the head, or gut, or legs, or neck, and cough and fell into a pool of blood and choked on it. Blood ran through the wood on our ship as some of our crew mates died on site, or were losing so much blood that they were close. Bullets hit the wood quickly. We fired back as much as we could, the sky a filled of smoke and fire and bullet. As bullets zipped over my head, canon balls hitting the ocean water near us, I saw the shovel gun further down. The shovel gun was a two barred canon that made it easier to target specific ranges.

"Cover me! I'm going to make a sprint to the shovel!" I yelled at Daniel and Tim as bullets fired overhead.

Daniel stood up and fired his musket hitting a man on the ship across. His body plummeted into the water. I shot up and sprinted towards the small canon across the deck. The bullets hit up the wood in front of me as I ran, carrying my musket at my side. Canon balls whipped by my body barely missing me and I could feel the wind of them. I hit the deck, and pulled out a crate of two chained canon balls together. I stuffed them in the hole and lit the match. I aimed it at the mast. The canon fired and the chained tethered balls spun towards the ship. I watched it clipped the tallest mast and snap it in two. I heard the sailors scream in terror as it came down, like a creaking giant, the red sails shot towards our ship. The mast smashed into the ocean creating a big ocean spray onto our deck, and the mast creating a bridge across to the other ship.

"Henry!" Tim shouted over canon fire.

"Charge lads! Give me what for!" Samuel yelled over the fire of bullets.

I reloaded my musket and we all charged over the wooden bridge of the mast. The ocean roared beneath my feet as I took careful step. The other crew still fired, knocking some of the crew in a cloud of red into the water. Samuel lead the way and tackled a man once he got aboard. Daniel aimed his blunder buss and fired the gun. It echoed through the sky with a big roar, and many bullets shot out and sprayed into five sailors and they died in their own guts.

Just before I jumped down from the tall mast, as my crew mates pushed past me, and charged into the fight, swords clashing and musket ball flying in a hand to hand combat of fists and blood, I aimed my sights at a sailor and fired hitting him between the eyes. The bullet shot through the bridge of his nose making them back of his head split open on either side like a cape. I jumped down and didn't have time to reload. I charged in, and shoved my bayonet into the gut of a man, whose blood gurgled out of his mouth and he fell dead at my feet. I then turned to my right to see a man swing his cutlass at my face. I turned my gun sideways, holding it both in my hands, and put it up above as a block. He slashed his sword downward and collided with my gun. I pushed the gun upwards and pushed the man backwards. He swung again, but this time, I deflected it with my bayonet. The sword flew sideways and I flipped the gun into the air and caught it by the butt and smacked him in the jaw making his teeth fly high into the sky. He stumbled over board into the water. I then turned a full 360 spin and hit a man in the head with my gun. I then looked to my left and saw a man heading for my gut. He swiped to my gut but I jumped to my right dodging it barely. The blade swished by my belly softly, and I gripped my musket and hit them man in the head making him collapse. I dropped my gun, and pulled out my cutlass from its sheath hearing it ring as it came too. I gripped the silver blade as it shined in the sunlight, its golden hilt firm in my hand. I looked to my left to see Daniel laughing with blood on his face, stabbing a man in the back. Tim had been firing his gun at many sailors making them drop dead, but soon he switched to his sword and was in a heated sword fight. The Captain was by the wheel sword fighting the captain. Each side of the sailors were clinging swords together in a face to face combat full or swords, muskets fire, punches, kicks, choking, and stabbing. Blood leaked under my boots, and bodies were everywhere, guts spilled over the crates and sides.

I heard a sailor heading my way and I slashed my sword cutting him down with one fatal blow. I then collided swords with a man, hearing the iron clinks and seeing it spark when the swords crossed.

We clashed swords together three more times pacing back and forth. He swung to my left but I ducked and pushed him down and shoved my blade into his stomach. I began to drag it up through his stomach, as blood spray out and his intestines piled out, he screamed in pain and died from the pain.

I turned around and collide swords with another sailor. He slashed at my arm, cutting into it, and creating a large gash across it. I screamed in pain and stumbled back, as blood poured from my white sleeve. I growled and knocked his sword from his hands. His eyes widened with fear as he turned away and tried to run to jump over the edge. He began to run but I chased after him. I slashed my sword at the back of his neck, the back of his neck splitting open like a Devil's grin, and he tumbled over the edge dead.

I charged deeper into the maze, slashing down sailors and dodging pistol fire as bullets rang hitting some of my own comrades into a blood pool. Just then, I was shoved down, my sword scattering across the deck away from me. The man climbed on top of and raised his sword high ready to plunge it deep into my heart.

"Henry catch!" I heard Daniel scream.

Within a second, he threw me a iron sword. Just before the sword was going to stab me, I caught the hilt gripped the blade with my right hand and the hilt with left hand. I held it in a line, and the enemy sword clashed down onto mine and sparks flew. Our swords locked together, his was weighing down on me. I then saw his hips were spread apart, and I kicked him in the balls. He yelped and dropped away his blade. I sliced off his head and blood rained down on my hands and face covering it completely. I leaned over and pushed his headless body off me. I threw up, and wiped the blood from my eyes and face. I stood up, and saw Samuel stab then Captain and chop off his head. The crew men saw their Captain defeated they surrendered. Samuel raised his bloody sword high into the air.

"Aye!" He bellowed.

"Aye!" We all yelled raising our weapons.

Only 15 sailors were left. We collected their booty, and stuffed it under our deck. We took the 15 prisoners, and burned the ship into flames watching it sink beneath the waves. Once the German ship bubbled beneath the ocean, we counted our dead which was 60 casualties.

"60 men." Samuel muttered. "Tragedy."

Our crew was only 70 men now. The 15 survivors of the attack, were lined on the top deck, all their hands bound behind their backs. Most of their clothes were bloody and torn or singed. My clothes and hands were covered in red as well as Daniels and Tim's and most of the crew. Blood ran down the wood of our ship. There were some holes in the sides and the main mast, but our ship would pull through. We placed our lost friends in a green cloth and tossed them over into the sea for burial.

After that, Samuel faced the prisoners. "Now, who can tell me why you decided to attack a supply ship?"

The prisoners exchanged looks of confusion. One of the prisoners in anger yelled at Captain Samuel. "Nien!" (No!)

"Well that wasn't very nice." Samuel frowned. He pulled out his pistol, cocked it and shot them man in the chest. The bullet wen straight through, and the prisoner sat up on his knee's for a second, eyes filled with shock, mouth wide open. He them tumbled over to his side, blood dripping out. Two of our men grabbed him and tossed him over the ship into the ocean.

"That is what happens when you don't listen. I'm going to ask you again, why did you attack our supply ship?" Samuel said more firmer.

Again the prisoners frowned, not responding. Samuel sighed. "Do they speak English?" Tim asked.

"I don't think so." I said.

"DANIEL!" Samuel shouted which startled Daniel. Daniel trotted over with the blunder buss.

"Yes sir." Daniel said.

"Do you speak German?" He asked.

"Aye sir I do." Daniel smiled.

"Perfect. Now, tell these lads, if they want to live they will explain why they attacked my ship." Samuel said.

"Aye Captain." Daniel said and walked up to one of the prisoners.

He stood before them, gripping his blunder buss, and letting the prisoners know what he means.

"Warum hast du das Schiff von Kapitän Samuel angegriffen?"(Why did you attack Captain Samuels ship?) Daniel asked them.

"Wir wussten nicht, dass es ein Versorgungsschiff war." (We didn't know it was a supply ship.) A prisoner responded.

"What did he say?" Samuel asked as the whole crew stood behind him.

Daniel turned to him. "He said they didn't know we were a supply ship."

Samuel sighed again. "I hardly believe that. Tell them I don't believe his word and if he doesn't tell me the truth, I will shoot him."

Daniel nodded. He turned to the man who spoke. "Der Kapitän glaubt dir nicht. Er fragt noch einmal: Warum haben Sie unser Schiff angegriffen? Wenn Sie nicht antworten, wird er Sie erschießen." (He doesn't believe you. The Captain asks again: Why did you attack our supply ship? Answer or he'll shoot you.).

The prisoner shook in fear. He spoke but his voice was shaky. "Ich sage die Wahrheit. Wir wussten es nicht. Es waren unsere Kapitänsbefehle." (I'm telling the truth. We didn't know. It was our captains orders.)

"Daniel?" Samuel asked.

"He said he's speaking the truth. They didn't know, they were just follow orders." Daniel said.

"Something isn't right here." Tim muttered to me.

"What?" I asked.

"They would know we were a supply ship, we were flying our colors." Tim said.

"I think he's lying." Samuel said sternly.

Daniel turned to the prisoner. "Er denkt, dass Sie lügen." (He thinks you're lying.)

The prisoner shook his head. "Ich bin nicht ly-" (I'm not ly-)A bullet flew into his head and he toppled over. I looked at Samuel who blew the smoke off the muzzle.

"13 prisoners left. Come on lads, tell me the truth or I'll feed you too the sharks!" Samuel screamed.

"Sagen Sie ihm die Wahrheit." (Tell him the truth). Daniel said.

"Fick dich!" Two of the prisoners yelled.

"What's that mean?" I asked.

"They said...Fuck you." Daniel said.

Samuel smiled coldly. "Okay, enough. Excuse them lads, and toss em over into the blue. Henry and Tim, a few injured sailors are below the deck, go help the doctor. Daniel and a few others kill them." And walked below deck. Daniel nodded and shot the prisoners one by one and the bodies were tossed over board. Me and Tim ran down below deck tossing our muskets by our hammocks. We pushed past below deck and slammed through two doubled wooden doors below deck. Once us two entered I was in shock at what I saw. The entire room was red. Blood ran down through the cracks between the wood of the ship. Injured sailors of at least 20, were screaming on poorly looking tables and counters. A doctor in a white trench coat and spectacles was attending a sailors leg pouring some liquid on the festering pus wound. He looked at us up from the leg, pushing his glasses up from his nose, getting blood smudges on them. Bones laid around the floor and there was so much blood it was ungodly.

"What are you two doing down here?" The doctor shot at us with a squeaky voice.

"The captains sent us down here to help you." I said.

"OH, well, good I could use some help. How many are dead? What is the casualty report?" The doctor asked.

"60." Tim sadly said.

"My god, bless there souls." He prayed. "Now, do hurry, help me with this man."

The doctor ushered me and Tim over to a table to our left. A man was laying there with his shirt ripped off. Blood covered his chest and face, and arms, and legs. He was out.

"Is he dead?" Asked Tim.

"No, just out cold. Help me with his leg." The doctor fumbled with his glasses.

I looked at his leg which was broken. The shin bone was split in half and popping above the skin. Pus and blood mixed together leaked out of the red wound. I began to get dizzy just looking at it. Tim threw up on his own boots. "I can't look." He coughed.

The smell in this room was awful. Full of shit, piss, blood, and pus, no man should ever have to stand this, even the lowest of men.

"You have too son. Look, I need to chop off his leg, it's infected. He was shot in the leg and the ball shattered his bone and shin. He won't be able to walk on it again. First I need to get the ball out to stop him from getting infected and them remove it." The doctor said.

"Good thing he's out cold for this." Tim muttered.

"Yes." The doctor laughed.

The doctor quickly grabbed some giant metal twitters. "Henry, hold down his leg, just under his knee."

I gulped and gripped just under his knee and holding down his leg firmly.

"Great, now, Tim I need you to peel back his open flaps of skin so I can get a good view of where the musket ball is, so I can try to get it out." The doctor said.

Tim looked at him and then me. He groaned and slowly reached his hands out. He reached for the unconscious man's shin that was open. He gripped the bloody layers of skin and peeled it back, it squished as he pulled it back. Tim was about to throw up again and so was I. When Tim peeled it back, the bone sticking out was more visible and I could make out the blue and red arteries and veins in the leg. The doctor stuck the metal in the man's leg and fumbled around in the wound. He pricked a piece of bone and tossed it out on the floor. He then finally found the ball and pulled out the crumpled piece of bloody metal and put it in a metal cup.

"Perfect, now, I'm going to remove his right leg. Henry, hold his leg steady." The doctor pleaded.

I nodded. I gripped the man's leg tightly as the doctor grabbed a big bloody saw blade. The saw had razor sharp edges on the blade and a cracked wooden handle on the back. The doctor nudged his spectacles with the saw still in his hand. He slowly placed it just above the skin and bone of his right leg.

"Ready?" The doctor asked.

We both nodded. He began to saw into the leg cutting past the skin like it was paper. He then cut through the veins, popping the blood vessels making the blood gurgle out of the wound. He then started to pierce the sinews, slicing through the veins and arteries. He then set the saw blade down, and reached in the wound and yanked out a few veins letting them spill onto the table. Tim stared at them and puked again. I kept my eyes looking down at my boots. He cut a few more pieces of meat off. He got to the white bone and the saw got stuck in the middle of the bone. He set the saw down.

"Henry, hand me that hammer." He said.

I saw a small mallet laying on the table a few yards away from me. I picked it up and tossed it to the doctor who caught it.

"Tim, hand me that pike next to you please." The doctor begged with his red hands.

My hands and Tim's were splotched stained with blood. Tim grabbed the giant iron spike and gave it to the doctor.

"Thank you men." He said.

He placed the pike on top of the bone, right in the middle of the shin. He raised the hammer and cracked it down. The bone cracked, split in half. The bone severed in the wound. The doctor picked up the bones and threw it out.

Seeing the bone being thrown out, made my legs wobbly. Then the doctor sawed into the rest of the bone making pieces give way. He then cut back into the flesh, and then with one last fatal hack, chopped of the man's right leg and it toppled to the floor covered in blood. The leg started to become purple and black. The doctor picked it up and tossed it in a wooden barrel full of arms, hands, legs, and body parts. The body parts sat in some redish green liquid in the barrel. The doctor took off his glasses and cleaned them with a cloth, and washed his hands in a bucket.

"Now, come on. I need your help with one more thing." He muttered towards me and Tim.

He ushered us two over to a man who was still present. The man's left arm was completely destroyed. His bone, flesh, and veins were everywhere and he had been shot with a blunder buss, and it tore up his arm. He had to lose it.

"I need to remove his arm. I ran out of morphine, so I need you to hold him down as I do this." The doctor looked at us both seriously.

Me and Tim exchanged looks and walked over to the man. He was screaming from the pain already in his arm but removing it would be worse. The doctor wiped the saw with a rag and tossed the bloody rag to the floor. He placed the saw on the arm.

"Henry and Tim, hold him down now." The doctor said.

We compiled and did so. I gripped down his shoulders, giving him a piece of wood to bite down on between his teeth. His eyes frantically looked around the room and up at us.

"Doc, Doc, let me keep it!" The sailor screamed.

"I can't, I'm sorry, it's already infected by the bullet, if I let you keep your arm the infection will spread and kill you." The doctor said.

Tim held down his arm. The poor man looked into my eyes and I had no choice but to avert mine. The doctor drove the blade deep into the arm, cutting up the flesh and bone. The man screamed in agony as the blade cut deeper and deeper into his left arm. I couldn't imagine the pain this man was in. The man's body shivered and thrashed like a fish out of water. I had to grip tighter on both of his shoulders from squirming. The sailor bit down on the wood, cutting his teeth up and tongue. He bit down so hard that the wood split in half. The doctor cut his arm clean off and the man's eyes rolled into his head and he stop moving. The doctor tossed the arm into the bin.

"Is he...dead?" Asked Tim.

"No, just in shock. He'll be alright." The doctor said breathing heavy.

"Thank you for helping me but I think I have it from here."

"Of course." I smiled and me and Tim began to head towards the door until the doctor stopped me. He gripped my right arm. I winced in pain.

"Your cut sir." The doctor said.

I looked down at my arm to see a wide red gash on it from the sword. I was so enthralled by amputation procedure I had completely forgotten about it.

"It's just a simple cut." I said.

"Yes, but it will get infected and you don't want to lose your arm right?" He asked.

I looked at Tim and then the doctor and nodded for him to clean it. The doctor grabbed a clean rag and wiped away the blood. Once that was done he mushed up some mint leafs and stuffed them into my cut. I winced in pain since it stung but overall I was alright. After he was done I thanked the doctor and me and Tim headed out. Within the hour, we had changed into fresh new clothes, and washed the blood of our bodies. After that, we headed for Captain Samuel's quarters.

Once we entered the captains cabin, we saw Samuel furiously fiddling with the map, looking for routes for Germany. Daniel was not here, so I assumed he was still getting cleaned up.

"Sir?" I asked.

He looked up from the map, the blood from his sword fight with the German captain still was on his shirt.

"Those damnable prisoners knew more than what they were telling us." He trembled with rage.

"Aye sir, I sniffed some betrayal in the air." Tim said.

"Betrayal?" Samuel asked astonished.

"Aye Captain." Tim said.

"Well, master Tim, enlighten me will you?" Samuel asked the young man, sitting down in his chair.

Tim looked at me and then back at the Captain. "I think I know who sent that ship."

"You do?" Samuel asked.

"I'm not a hundred percent certain, but I have a feeling it was Colin Baggins." The young man muttered.

"Baggins? Why on earth would he target me? We are long life friends." Samuel explained.

"He knows we are carrying much valuable supplies on board. He knew that about this ship. You even said he sometimes is a sleek one. I just sensed something was off. He sent the German ship to try and sink us, and then would collect the supplies afterward." Tim explained to the captain.

The captain leaned back in his chair with a look of shock. "Timothy, there is one thing to assume such, but to assume my long life friend, that is ungodly!" His fists trembled with rage.

"But sir-" Tim said but the captain suddenly threw his maps off the table in anger.

"But nothing master Timothy! We are on route to Germany! We need to get theses supplies in fast or we will be in dire trouble with the Duke of England. Now, we were attacked and our ship is damaged, lost half my crew! Damn!" He cried in anger falling into his chair as a defeated man.

Tim stood there a little shell shocked. I as well. We just stood there in silence as the Captain huffed and puffed in anger. The crumpled maps laid on the wood floor. He put his hand on his face stroking his beard.

"I'm sorry lads, just this attack has set us backwards." He mumbled.

"I understand sir. No offense taken." Tim said.

"Good. Now, did you check the supplies before coming to me?" Samuel asked me and Tim.

"Uh, no sir, we have not." I said quickly.

"Why not?" He asked.

"Well, you sent us to help the doctor with the injured men." I said.

"Oh that's right, you were helping the doctor. How many dead from the injuries?" He asked.

"Only a few." Tim said.

"Dammit. I'm losing too many good men." Samuel frowned. He stood up and gathered his fallen papers and placed them back on the desk. He scanned the giant map before him and opened up his log book.

"What's the date?" He asked.

"June 14, 1679, it's a Thursday." I said.

"Thank you Henry." He said recording it in his leather log book. "And where is Daniel?"

Daniel stumbled into the captains quarters. He was cleaned up from the fight. His black hair was curly and low, and his green eyes showing shock.

"I'm sorry sir, I was getting cleaned up." He mumbled.

"It's alright, now, the prisoners in the sea?" He asked.

"Yes sir, with the sharks." Daniel said.

"Wonderful." Samuel smiled with joy.

"Uh, sir I have something to show you." He muttered.

"What is it?" Asked Samuel.

Daniel staggered over to the captain and pulled out a small piece of paper, damaged by water. He unrolled it, and let Samuel look at it. After a minute of pause, he set the paper down on his desk and I could see his hands trembling with fury, his eyes full of hate and anger, his whole body was shaking.

"Son of a bitch! That bastard!" Samuel cried as his angry voice screamed through the ship, as it rocked through the waters.

"I found it off one of the dead prisoners." Daniel told us.

"What is it?" I asked walking over to the desk.

I picked up the ruined piece of paper. In ink it read: *"Sink the Deltarone to the depths. Report back to me after done back in Dublin, and I will come to collect and you all will get a share. -Colin."*

My heart thumped angrily, and my eyes widened with shock. Tim hurried over and read it and had the same look as me.

"Colin ordered this?" I asked.

"Aye. That slick bastard, he always a crafty one." Samuel muttered. "But we bested him." Samuel then looked at Tim. "I'm sorry lad, I should have trusted your word."

"It's alright captain." Tim said.

"Should we change course back to Dublin, to get Colin?" I asked the captain. Captain Samuel stared down at his desk with anger filling up his hot blood.

"No, we first go get the mermaid. Then back to Dublin. The mermaid is more important. I'll let him bask in his own filthy glory thinking he sank us down, and then when he least excepts it, we will strike."

In the Middle of the African ocean
July, 1679
Longitude and Latitudes Unknown

A month had passed since the attack from Captain Baggins and we haven't seen his ship or crew anywhere. We are lost somewhere off the Horn of Africa in the middle of the ocean. No ships are in sight. Heat is hitting our heads hard, making us weaker and more tired.

The sun is unforgiving, baking down on us like cooked fish. The planks of the ship were boiling hot under our boots, even the nails between the boards were sizzling. Sweat drenched our bodies and we were sweating so much, we had more of that too drink then fresh water.

Captain Samuel has been mainly in his cabin, with the aid of Daniel occasionally wrapping around the Horn. I knew we were close to Madagascar but no islands were in sight. Our supplies was low and some of the injured from the battle a month ago, were apart of the deep now. The crew was now only at 48 men strong.

The boat rocked aimlessly in the ocean waters, no wind was blowing to carry her forward and we were just drifting slowly, rocking back and forth.

Me, Daniel, and Tim sat under the main mast, that gave us a little shield from the sun. Two other sailors were with us and one of them being a young man around Tim's age. His name was William Pett, a mighty young lad that was always on crows nest duty, so his home was the crows nest more than his actually hammock below deck.

He had short brown hair, and a thick beard across his face. His brown eyes sat like almonds in his sockets as he eyed his cards. We were playing a round of cards, betting on a few gold coins. A pile of gold sat in the middle of our circle.

I looked at my group of cards. They aren't a paid play, having a ace, kings and queens and a ten of diamonds. Tim and Daniel carefully set a five of spades and six of clubs down on the ground.

"Aye, be careful what you put down." William laughed.

"Oh shut your trap and gawk Will. I know what I'm doing." Tim blundered.

I grinned under my cards as I held them up. I looked at the circle of my friends. I had a good play, I could win this money.

"Alright, one at time flush the cards out." Daniel said.

The other man flushed his out on the planks showing a poor count. He groaned and threw the cards down and left. Tim flushed his out, showing three tens and an ace. It was good but not good enough.

"Fuck." He groaned in frustration.

"Aye, Timothy, looks like the tens got the best of ya." Daniel laughed.

"Damn cards. I was for sure I'd beat you lassies." Tim said.

"Not smart enough." I laughed.

Daniel flushed his out revealing a set of mighty red and black cards. He had two kings, a queen but two four of clubs. William grinned and revealed his which was three kings, and a queen. Daniel groaned plopping his cards down.

"Better luck next time Dan." William snickered.

"Stop popping and let's see what Henry has." Daniel said.

I eyed William and I could see a tinge of worry in his face. I grinned over the rim of my five cards. I saw his and if it wasn't for mine he would have won but the card set I had was a royal flush.

"Royal Flush." I smiled slapping my cards on the deck.

Daniel, Tim, and even some of the crew laughed. William flared up in frustration. "You cheater. I have never seen anyone get a royal."

I collected the coins and slipped them in my pocket. "Luck I guess."

"Luck ain't the half of it. You cheated." William pouted as I stood up.

"Oh stop puckering your lip Will, Henry, won fair and play." Tim said.

I grinned and flicked William two coins. "There."

William grinned and stood up gripping the two coins. "I suppose it was luck."

"Aye." I smiled.

After the card game, Will and Tim went over and surveyed the shipments of black powder to make sure it was accounted for. Daniel went over to edge of the boat and pulled out a wooden rusty pipe. He stuffed some tobacco inside and struck the match on the side of the boat. He put the match in the hole and puffed out with his mouth creating white smoke.

I walked over to the edge of the boat beside him. He rested both hands on the edge, half hanging off the edge above the water. The boat swayed slightly side by side, no wind pushing the sails. The heat pierced down on us. I pulled out a water cask and finished off the remaining cool water I had. I then slipped some chew into my mouth and spit into the water.

"Fresh water is running low." Daniel said to me still keeping his eyes on the water.

I leaned my back against the stern of the boat, looking out at Tim and Will laughing at some seagulls that kept pooping on the sails.

"I know. Supplies of food and powder are low as well." I said worried.

Daniel looked at me. "Good play."

"Aye, I knew what I was doing." I grinned.

"Clearly." Daniel said.

Daniel sucked the smoke and blew it out of his mouth. The tip of the pipe burning with a red flame casting white smoke into the air from the front hole.

"Samuel is getting worried. We don't know where we are, and we're off course. Crew's getting mighty feisty too." Daniel said.

I nodded. "Aye. Were off the course."

Daniel leaned on one elbow and faced me. "You really believe that mermaid banter the Captain has been spitting in our ears?"

I stood there for a minute thinking it over. "As of now, I'm unsure. If he's wrong will still get a cut of coin." I paused for a minute. "But..."

"But?" Daniel asked.

"But if he's right. We could discover something truly magnificent." I smiled.

"Right you are." Daniel smiled.

The boat churned sides into the waves with a big creak as I fell backwards onto my back. Daniel toppled to his side, his pipe falling over the ship. The whole boat shook and most of the crew hit the ground with thuds. Under the ship I could hear the wood crack.

I reached up and grabbed the side of the boat and hauled myself up to peer over the edge. The crew did the same. I gazed down to see under the water it was bubbling white but I couldn't see past the surface.

"What in gods name was that?" Tim shouted.

"We must have hit a reef!" A sailor yelled up to the crows nest man.

"We need to rear the boat to starboard side!" Cried another.

Captain Samuel rushed out form below deck. "What did we hit?" He yelled as he ran over and look over the rim.

"A reef we think sir." Daniel said.

"A reef? Are you sure?" Samuel asked Daniel.

"I'm not sure sir." Daniel muttered.

Captain Samuel groaned and looked up at the crows nest. He cupped his hands to his mouth. "Can you see what we hit sir?" His voice echoed up high. It took a second for the man to respond but his response was lost in the wind. Samuel repeated again. "Say again?"

"It's not a reef!" Cried the crows nest man.

"What do you mean?" I asked.

Suddenly, a giant tentacle shot up from the waves. The tentacle raised high way above the rim of the Deltarone. It's tentacle was massive. The tentacle reached well over the boat. It's pink suckers and green lime slimly skin above it's meaty eight arms were colossal. Each sucker was the size of a rowboat, and lengthy in size. I heard the creature roar under the waves and I peered over the rim. Under the surface of the water, was a monstrous creature. It's eight giant tendrils were holding onto the bottom of the wood ship. It's dark yellows placed on either side of its head stared up through the glassy foam up at me. His gaping sharp jaws snapped open and closed revealing a mouth of deadly force.

"Kracken!" Screamed a sailor and started to ring the bell as the bell echoed in my ears.

"Arm yourself! Hurry!" Captain Samuel screamed and rushed to the wheel climbing up the stairs hopping up them two at a time.

The tendril swung downward slamming into a few iron canons. The canons snapped from their ropes. The iron clad contraptions tumbled over ramming into a few sailors killing them instantly on impact, guts and blood flew like spice. Blood sprayed onto the deck. The tendril slung its meaty suckers towards a few sailors swiping them off their feet and over into the sea.

I watched in horror as two more tendrils rose from the water making salt water rain down on us drenching our clothes and faces. I spit the water from my mouth tasting salt and seaweed. I watched as they slammed down on the front deck of the ship. The ship turned downward dipping sideways to the left. Me and Daniel hit under the rim of the ship. I saw a few sailors scream and stumble, slipping down the deck and fall into the water, disappearing into the hissy jaws of the creature. I gulped. As the Deltarone started to tip over sideways from the left, I watched Tim and William tumble, literally falling in mid air towards us. Tim smacked his side against the hull as Will plopped into Daniel making Daniel wince. The boat groaned as the wood popped and riveted. Nails began to pop up from the planks making the whole ship start to sink sideway, the right side almost facing straight up. I peered at the wheel seeing Samuel hang on for dear life trying to turn the wheel starboard and back up.

I peered up to see barrels, supplies, guns, and canons, canon balls tumble down the deck flying past us into the water. I then heard a rope snap and saw a huge iron canon tumbled and rolling towards me and Tim.

"Oh shit!" I screamed. "Tim!"

I gripped Tim's shoulders and rolled along the edge of the boat as the iron beast flew at lightening speed towards my body. The iron missed my body by inches and smashed a hole into the rim of the boat creating a opening in the ocean. The canon smacked onto a tendril of the beast and it echoed in pain letting go of the ship, The ship shot back upright and we tumbled to the deck. Holes of the wood and half of our supplies was at the deep along with some men.

"Load the guns! Hurry lads! It's gonna strike again!" Samuel echoed loading his pistol.

"The guns! There under the deck!" Will yelled.

We and the crew popped up and began running towards the lower deck. The giant squid, raised it's tendrils and struck again. As my feet slapped down the stairs men were running all around gather weapons under the deck. I watched as the tentacles smacked through the woods under the deck, taking out the canons and men. As we ran across the deck, canon balls and canons, guns, men sailed over our-heads, water sprayed on our faces. The beasts screamed in anger. A rope full of explosives was taken down by three of the pink tendrils. It exploded into a fire of orange creating a hole blast in the side of the ship. As I saw the barrel of muskets in the back, a tendril swooped for me. I ducked hitting the wood floor lined with wet water and blood and slime. A man to my right was grabbed and drug out. He screamed for us to help him as he was being taken to the deep. The pink suckers kept him held tight as the tendril pulled out of a canon hole hatch making a sucking sound that was awful. The sailor screamed as half of his body, head to torso fit through but his legs still hung upside down in the ship. I heard his back crack in half and his legs go limp and he was sucked through the canon hole. I gulped and looked Daniel, Tim, and Will. We stood up and made it to the weapons. I loaded the musket and we headed back on deck to see a battle. Eight nasty tendrils were being swung around the deck, smashing into crates, tearing the ship literally in half. The ship creaked under the waves as it popped and gave way. Sailors were being gripped by the squid and being thrown off the ship as other fired the musket balls into the flesh of the beast making it cry in pain. Blood from the beast splattered on the deck. Samuel held the helm spinning the wheel round and round, creating a powerful spin on the ship. Supplies, canons, crates, guns, men, were being flown everywhere as salt water rained down.

I aimed down the sights and shot a tendril making a small bloody hole. It screamed and twirled its tentacle up trying to heal it but we kept shooting at it creating more blood. Slime lined the deck. William and Tim ran down the deck firing their guns at the monster. Daniel hurried over to a still strapped down canon and loaded a canon ball in. He aimed it at the squid, lining it up. The canon fired with blue smoke, and the ball teared it's tendril off. It yelled as blood bubbled up and its tentacle ducked under the waves. I fired my musket again seeing the bullet hit its target. I peered up at the crows nest to see that I could get a advantage point on the giant squids head. I strapped my musket across my chest and began climbing up the rope, as canon balls and musket fire rang out below the deck of screaming men. The ship tossed and turned side to side but she held her own from the beast.

I gripped the ropes, hearing the explosion down below. I was halfway up the mast, when I could see the creature under the water. Its eye glared at me with rage. I loaded the gun and held on the rope aiming down the sights. I popped off another shot but missed. I strapped my gun across my shoulder and kept climbing. The monster hit the side of the ship sending a man tumbling over the edge to his death.

I lost my grip and fell a few feet but caught the rope just in time. I gulped, my heart racing I kept climbing. Tim and William were at the front bow, firing off muskets and throwing flaming torches at the beasts to try to scare it off but it wasn't doing much. Daniel had helped from the crew as they fired the canon balls into the beast creating a line of blood and slime and pink sucker flesh. Captain Samuel kept the boat steady as much as he could as it rocked in the waves violently.

I made it at top the crows nest and aimed down the sight with the gun. I fired the ball and it hit in straight in one of its yellow eyes. It screamed in such pain it smashed against the boat. I lost my balance and dropped my musket off the nest and it plummeted into the waves below. I slipped falling backwards off the crows nest. As I fell, I flipped out a small knife from under my belt and stabbed it into the white sail as I slid down it. The knife cut through it like silk and drag down as I still slid. Finally, the knife stuck to the rope and I was jerked to a stop and fell to the deck hitting my back with a hard thud.

"Fire!" Samuel cried.

I was beside the cannons all five of them lined up. All the crew lit the match and the canons fired the ball. The iron balls pierced the tendrils of the beast ripping them apart in a cloud of green slime and red blood. I covered my ears to the loud sound of canon fire. Once the smoke cleared the tendrils plopped below the waves and the squid sunk into the depths lifeless.

We all cheered that we defeated the kraken and that the Deltarone was still intact and floating still. It took us a few minutes to recover from that blow. There no bodies since the beast had eaten them in one bite. Samuel had us sweep off the blood and green slime from the giant octopus with brooms and clear it off with soap and water. The wood soaked wet in the hot sun, parts of the ship were missing. Parts of the stern, and front were completely gone, and lower there some blows to the bottom. Samuel had surveyed the crew and we were 27 remaining. The Captain was upset for losing so many men to a sea creature, and he felt like he wasn't prepared for this.

We were lost, survived a brutal attack, that destroyed the ship mostly, and took half the crew, and we were low on supplies. Samuel looked high up into the clouds which were dark grey.

"God be with us." He frowned and went below deck.

Part 3

A New Eden

I awoke startled to a crash of thunder outside. I sat up in my hammock and it swayed as I carefully place my bare feet on the wood. Crew men were rushing around up the deck and below. I slipped on my boots and flipped on a frock coat and hurried up to the deck. Once I broke into the air, it was night out, and the wind howled. Thunder cracked through the grey clouds creating a white flash in the night sky. Rain hailed down on us as waves of hundreds of feet tall crashed up onto the deck creating a small pond of water.

I peered up holding on to my cap from the wind and salt rain as Samuel steered the boat deep towards the waves. Thunder rang out continuously every few minutes and echoed through the sea. I saw the crew struggling to tighten down our few remaining canons and supply crates.

 Never have I wished so much for the land, to feel the sweet brown soils of home. For on this sea I could feel the rage within, as if the ocean is countless tears ready to pound at the feet of man, to teach he who has wanted yet not nurtured as he should. It is a gale that screams under dark and serious clouds. Yet the boat sails over these watery fists, perhaps with the intention of causing enough bruising for the sailors to remember her anger, enough for them to start a sweet serenade of sorrow and a promise of better care.

Waves crashed up onto the deck making the sailors slip under their feet.

"Lad help me with this!" Daniel yelled over the rain.

Thunder shot out creating another white light in the night sky as I ran over to him. I slipped hitting the deck from the water pouring over the rims. The boat rocked violently back and forth in the waves. We went up a big wave and pounded down, as I gripped on the side of the boat to keep steady. I landed near Daniel and helped him fastened down the crates. He tossed me aside rope and I pulled it across the top of the lids.

The gulls are tossed paper in a storm, flashes of white in the grey, tumbling as they struggle against the gale. Beneath them the sea rises as great mountains, anger in the form of water, turbulent and unforgiving.

On this sea we sailors try to prepare for sudden, violent storms, but we knew it was impossible. The worst has happened tonight; with no warning, total darkness prevailed as clouds thickened and the sky was stricken, blotting out the moonlight and stars. The wind arose to push the still waters to choppy, which morphed into mountains of angry waves. Four sailors across from me struggled to get the sails down, and to tie them off. They slipped on the rain soaked deck. When the other men of the crew heard and saw how frightened the sailors were, they panicked. The wind slammed the rain into our faces like tiny stones and pushed my cap off. The ship pressed, first up waves at forty-five degrees, and then crashed down jarring my bones. At one point the waves spun the vessel sideways. I held tightly onto the mast, onto ropes, onto anything. It was difficult to hang on. A bolt of lightning struck near hitting the deck a few feet from me. My teeth bounced together from the blast.

"Call the Master! Where is the captain?!" someone shouted.

I looked up at the wheel to see Captain Samuel soaked in water, turning the wheel.

The boat hit the waves, ocean spray hitting up on the deck pouring in like a tidal wave.

The waves grew so large that the vessel was dwarfed, riding up and down the mighty swelling sea like a child's toy. Inside the ship there was no staying still unless the person was anchored in place, for the "floor" was whatever surface gravity flung the sailors upon. In that state I prayed to Poseidon himself.

There was no mercy in this hot wind, no grace in the waves, only wrath and tempest. The air was thick with a briny mist, the deck awash with salty waves. I felt coming the morning we would be bobbing on placid water or else several leagues down with the fishes.

"Cut the rowboats lose now!" Cried Samuel.

We crawled across the deck, and I pulled out a axe. I chopped down on the nasty rope hearing it snap free. The rowboats plummeted into the dark sea.

"Henry!" I heard Tim scream over the howling wind.

I slowly turned to see a giant wave, the biggest I had ever seen. It rose up to the heavens and began to crash down like sharp teeth. The Deltarone veered backwards tipping upward. I lost my balance and rolled down the deck flipping up past Samuel, who had fallen from the wheel. The whole crew tumbled backwards as the wave turned the ship straight up in the air and we toppled over upside down. My body hit the wood and then sank under the ocean water.

The wave current pushed me further and further down under the water as my lungs stung under the salty water. I peered below me to see some of the sailors sinking with the wreckage of her to the bottom. The boat was split in half completely.

I used all my strength and pushed my arms side to side and kicked up. I bursted into the rainy air gasping for air seeing no one in sight. The waves roared tossing me around in a whirlpool and would drag me up and under the water choking my lungs and giving me moments of air. The waves settled and the thunder cracked.

"Henry over here!" I heard a faint scream.

I peered to my left to see Tim and Daniel gripping onto a large piece of driftwood. I used all my strength and swam towards them. Tim reached out and pulled me onto the small drift wood.

"Glad to see you are alive gents!" I screamed over the screaming ocean and thunder.

"Aye lad! You too!" Daniel grinned.

"Where are the others?" Tim asked.

"Most of them have drowned!" I screamed. "She's gone mates! Sank under!"

I then heard another faint scream and gazed over the bobbing waves to see Captain Samuel and William Pett on another piece of plank.

I waved at them and they gave us a wave back. Samuel and Will pushed the wood over close to us as the rain poured down on us.

"Holy shit." Will said.

"Aye, we need to find the rowboats but I can't see em." Samuel muttered worried.

I gazed the dark waters of terrifying waves and couldn't see them anywhere. I looked up at the dark grey clouds seeing the lightening of white flash inside. I held onto the wood for dear life and prayed to God that I would survive this.

The next morning I woke up on the wood with Daniel and Tim. William and Samuel were with us as well. The waters were calm and still, and the sky blue. Before us was the wreckage of the ship. Crates bobbed in the water empty, while pieces of the ship bobbed as well. A few dead crew men were floating still on the surface. This driftwood was keeping us afloat it wasn't much and my fear not only grew for starvation but for sharks that lurk below.

I could see blood leaking from the dead bodies. I gulped. I gazed at the endless water and saw a rowboat floating silently a fifty yards or so away from us. Past the rowboat I could see land!

"Aye, look! Land Captain!" I pointed to the island in the distance.

"That must be Madagascar!" Samuel smiled happily. "And a rowboat!"

"God has answered my prayers!" William prayed.

"Come on lads, let's swim to her!" Tim smiled.

Tim was about to jump off the piece of wood but Daniel gripped his arm.

"Stop." Daniel muttered.

"Why? It's right there?" Will asked.

"William there-" Daniel pleaded but Will shook his head.

"It's right there and am I going for it laddies! I'll bring her round!" William laughed and dove into the ocean.

He sank under, kicked under water a couple feet away and came up for air and continued to form strokes to the rowboat.

"William!" Daniel yelled.

I then saw the dorsal fin. A gray thin line of a triangle cut through the silent water. I peered under the water to see the lifeless coal eye. It's sharp fangs set in its pink gums and large grey body swimming side to side with such grace.

"What?" William called.

126

"Shark!" Samuel yelled.

William's eyes went cold. The dorsal fin cut through the water, fast and disappeared under the water. The shark headed for Will. It was too late, he was too far. There was screaming as the big jaws opened wide and snapped shut on his gut. The teeth sank into his flesh. There was screaming, thrashing in the water, and then silence. An arm bobbed up from the waves and created a cloud of red in the water.

I shuddered in fear.

"My god." Tim shuddered.

Samuel gulped but noticed something. He pointed at the wooden rowboat away from us.

"Look, there is no way we will all make it if we swim now with sharks in the water. If we get Will's arm and toss it behind us, we should have time to make it. Help me paddle to the arm." Samuel muttered.

We agreed and used our arms to push the piece of driftwood closer to the limb. Once we got close enough, Daniel reached and picked it up. The arm was the only thing left of Will dripping blood.

"Poor lad." Daniel sadly said.

"Toss it." Samuel said.

Daniel chucked it behind us. The arm hit with a light splash and a minute later the shark smashed at it. Once that happened we all four dove into the water. My heart raced as my head went under and I used my arms to swim faster and faster to the rowboat. I came to the surface for air and kicked towards the boat. Tim was the first to make it and he climbed over board. Samuel was next and Tim lifted him up. I made it to the rowboat and grabbed Tim and Samuel's hand as they lifted me over. I plopped onto the wooden dingy, with a few oars laying about in the bottom.

Daniel kicked up the water and gripped the side of the boat with his legs still in the water. I looked up to see the shark was speeding towards Daniel with its jaws open.

'Daniel!" I cried.

Daniel yelped as I hauled him over just as the shark leaped above the water, its pink maw opened with razor sharp white teeth. Tim had grabbed a wooden oar and smacked it in the head making it topple over the side of the boat and sink below the depths dead. Tim huffed and puffed and set the oar down.

"Thanks for that." Daniel coughed out sea water.

"Don't mention it." Tim nodded.

We all collected ourselves and sat inside the small wooden dingy. Samuel pulled out his soaked map. He slapped it against the side of the ship and it tore in two and tumbled in the water and disappeared in small papery particles.

He dropped the remaining pieces into the ocean as the waves slapped up against the rowboat. Samuel rubbed his face in frustration, clasping his beard in his hand. He looked over his shoulder at his sunken ship.

"She was a good one sir." I said trying to bring up hopes.

He looked away from the wreckage and carnage what had occurred. The sun shone bright down on us casting a ember glow off the surface of the water.

"Aye, she was." He muttered softly.

Daniel clapped his shoulder. "Captain, I know it's a sad moment in these waters that are breathing, but." Daniel looked and pointed to the island.

"There is land. We need to make it there."

"Your right Master Daniel. Alright lads, let's get to rowing." Samuel nodded.

I picked up a wooden oar, as long as a fishing pole, with a thin shaft and a flat rectangular stub and drove it in the waves. The waves churned softly, as the supplies from the ship continuously floated by us. The sharks kept taking small bites from the remaining bodies of the dead crew, and dragged them beneath the surface to the deep. I peered over the rim of the rowboat, to see the ghastly grey fish swimming under us, there jaws snapping at the limbs. Other colorful fish of orange, blue, purple, and green swam with them in schools. Seahorses kicked on by as well. I used all my might and pushed the oar back and forth with Tim beside me doing the same. Samuel and Daniel were in front of us, backs facing us, digging their strength with the oars.

As we pushed the boat towards the land, the rowboat bounced up and down softly on the small calm waves. My heart was sinking to the pit of my stomach. Everything seemed to be going alright for us, until so many occurrences had struck us down. First the battle from that traitorous man Colin Baggins, then the kraken and know the storm and sharks, but God had shined down upon us with the island near.

I huffed out breath from my nostrils as I continued to sling the oar into the water as if I was cutting the water in half. After two hours we hit the edge of the island. We all hopped over the board, my boots hitting the shallow waters, soaking with salt, and we all pushed the boat ashore and stocked it still in the red sand.

I dropped the oar in the sand and fell on my back breathing heavy from all the rowing. My arms stung and throbbed in the sun and ached of pain. My legs felt wobbly and my eyes tired. We all collapsed on the red sand at the shore as the waves silently rolled up into the wet sand. After catching our breath and resting for a while, I sat up and checked myself. I had a bunch scraps and a giant bloody cut in the my side but it had stopped bleeding. I sighed with relief that the sharks decided to go for Will instead of me. I felt that my sword was still under my belt and my pistol was there too. I pulled it out and examined it. The polished wooden stock was wet and the trigger was slightly damaged. I checked the barrel and dumped the wet powder out. Luckily, I had a cask horn of the fresh powder and reloaded it with fresh dry powder and cocked the gun for safety.

We all collected ourselves and I gazed at the island.

"This is Madagascar." Samuel said. "The only place has red sand."

Tim crouched down and picked up a chunk of it. "It's so smooth."

"Aye, the cleanest of sands and clay lay here." Daniel said looking around.

The island was gorgeous. Red sands ran along the shore, and some of the supply crates had washed on the shore. With a smile of the sun on me and the abundance of sand surrounding me, I felt happy that we survived. The sand was smooth like glass paper and lying down on it felt like your back was on pillows. If the amount of sand on this island were rocks it would cover all of

Africa twice! The water around the island was as clear as glass and blue like the sky so the infinite depths of the sea were just a blink away. Fish small as rice grains flickered to and fro from the sandy beaches of the island to the cold gloomy depths of the sea.

Birds of large stature were abundant on this island. Their looming presence seemed to be the omen of dark intent as their dark sharp eyes stared at me with hunger and desire for human meat. The birds were distinguished easily as one type had bright orange and shiny blue feathers while the others had a mixture of grey and black feathers so when the light struck at different angles I saw the different colored feathers. Jungle stretched further in beyond us with large red clay mountains in the background.

" Oi boys the supply crates! There are some here!" Tim cried happily jumping up from the sand kicking it up from his boots as he ran.

We walked over and opened a few of the crates. Some water casks were still there filled with cold water. Rations of food such as dried meat, ripe fruit, and beans were there. Powder and pistol ball lay there too. We all smiled happily at the supplies.

"Thank you God for blessing us with this." Samuel looked up into the heavens. "Come on lads, let's drink before we decide what to do."

We drank the cold water it streamed down my throat with the cold refreshing sensation. My dry tongue and gums felt anew again, and we ate the dried meat until our bellies full. I felt my strength returning to my body. After we rested on the beach of red sand, the birds chirping above with cooing and whistles, Samuel gathered us up.

He pointed into the jungle. "I'm not exactly sure where is the exact place to where we will find a mermaid, but in the journals it said to look for a beautiful lagoon in the heart of the jungle"

"A lagoon?" I asked.

"Aye lad. Now we have our swords and pistols, take down anything that stands in our way." Samuel said sternly.

"Looking for a mighty blue lagoon. Got it." Tim said.

"Come on gents, into the jungle to become legends! Let's find a mermaid!"
Daniel cried happily.

"Well, how exactly do we plan to capture it?" I asked.

"Huh?" Samuel asked.

"Sir, how are we going to capture the creature?" I asked.

Samuel froze thinking hard. "Damn. Well, will think of something when the
time comes." He muttered. "Onward."

I pulled out my pistol, as Daniel and Tim and Samuel did the same. Samuel
also pulled out a giant sword and we trudged into the greenery. Once I
entered past giant palm leaves the size of rowboats, I was astonished by how
green this place was. The aura of the jungle, of a million wild souls, is as
tangible as water when one bathes. It is another sense, one that comes to the
heart rather than the eyes, as soaked in richness as they are.

Cutting our way through the dense, suffocating undergrowth, with our swords
fighting through the very air, which hung heavy, moist and still. Trees tall as
cathedrals surrounded us, and a strange green light - almost holy -
shimmered through the vast canopy of leaves. The rain forest seemed to have
an intelligence of it's own. It's voice was the sudden screech of a parrot, the
flicker of a monkey swinging through the branches overhead. It knew we were
here.

After a hour or so we had trudged onto the depth of the jungle, not finding
any human life or a lagoon in which we were told that holds a mythical
mermaid. We had been lucky so far. We had been attacked, of course, by
leeches and mosquitoes and stinging ants. We had to pick the leeches off our
skin as they sucked our blood from our flesh, smashed black scorpions, and hit
at ants that bite at us. The snakes had slithered past us, as long as a fishing
line, scaly black and yellow, their piercing eyes giving us way. We had
searched for about two hours and came up blank. I had kept my eyes peeled
for any movement of the such but it was hard to see anything through the
choking green.

The jungle was an assault on all senses. The virescent hues were the
foreground, the background and as high up as you could see. The heat and

humidity pressed in on my skin making sweat pointless. The sounds of the insects, the birds and the larger animals created a symphony of nature calling you deeper. The leaves brushed up against me and my feet sprung up with each step. The air tasted both sweet and fresh, like flowers blooming on my tongue.Colorful toucans with yellow pink beaks and black fur chirped in the branches of the twisted brown mangy forest.

Finally, we broke free from the humid forest, and bursted out into a wide open river. The river passed through the jungle wide and opaque. The water is green, darker in the shadows and more pale in the light, but still green. Against the noise of the birds that are welcoming the new day the gentle murmur of the water can only just be heard, a backdrop to the musical notes coming from above. For all its serenity there is more danger in its swirling depths than the trees behind I could fell. Between the crocs and the piranhas I don't even want to get my boots wet.

Samuel aimed his sword across the river. "We have to make it across."

"With what Samuel?" Daniel croaked. "We don't have a rowboat or a raft."

"Plus, I'm sure there are crocs and hippos that will tear our flesh." Tim muttered sweat dripping from his body.

Sweat trickled down my body like a waterfall. The birds called over ahead. The river current smashed agains the wet clay stones.

Samuel stomped over to Daniel, his boots soaked. "Have a better idea?"

Daniel laughed. "Captain Samuel, you are a swell captain but this is absurd."

"Absurd?" Samuel blinked twice.

"Aye! We are in the middle of a fucking jungle, lost, aimlessly searching for a creature that probably doesn't even exist! We are stranded, our ship in the depths, we are the only four remaining of our crew! Poor William was taken by the sharks. For all we know, we could be being hunted by a jaguar!" Daniel screamed over the roaring river.

Samuel's eyes danced with fury. "You offered to help me."

"We did sir, in good faith but Daniel is right. We need to stop living in this fantasy and we should look for a real way to save ourselves." I said.

"Sir we just need to rest and figure out what to do." Tim said.

Samuel laughed loudly. "Lads this is the truth! We are close I can sense it!"

I sighed and looked at the river of death. "Sir, we are going to die."

"Then we die!" Samuel cried. "I have to see this through. Look, there is some wet stones we can walk across, come on. Either you come with me, who knows what he's doing, or you be eaten."

I looked at Daniel and Tim sharing the same look of worry. We all three nodded and followed Samuel. We scooted down the edge of the muddy river bank and started to climb on top of the steps. As we shimmed across the rocks, I took careful steps to try not to slip off the wet moss. My boots slid and skidded softly as we stepped. The river pushed the rapids underneath us, making the current a death trap. Daniel was the first across. Then Samuel. Tim was close ahead of me but he slipped. His boots slapped off the rock and hit the water. He screamed as I dove and gripped onto his shirt collar. My belly skidded on the rocks as half of Tim's body was submerged in the river, as I'm holding him up with all my might.

"Shit!" I screamed as my arm was losing strength from the rapids.

I heard a shot of pistol ball hit the water next to Tim's feet. I gazed at Samuel's pistol smoking.

"What the fuck!" I screamed at Samuel as he fired a bullet near us. "Are you trying to kill us?!"

"No! Croc lads! Get up now!" Samuel's voice echoed down the rocks.

My eyes widened as I gazed past Tim's feet. I saw what looked like a log bobbing in the murky brown water. Then I saw the green eye souless as ever. The creature swam side to side, its small fat legs with claws slapping the river water. Me and Tim screamed in fear as the crocodile swam fast towards us, it's gaping mouth reaching wide open revealing a pink mouth and sharp white fangs. It hissed towards us as it came closer. With a quick movement, I pulled out my pistol, cocked it, and aimed with my free hand while my other held Tim up as half his body was under water.

The reptile launched up out of the water, its jaws wide open. It was a foot from snapping onto Tim's legs. I fired the bullet and it shot deep into the mouth of the beast. The croc spilled red blood from its gums and it somersaulted backwards doing a backflip and splashing into the water. It lay upside down floating dead and still.

I dropped my pistol and heaved Tim up and we hurried across the rocks falling onto the tall green grass on the other side of the river. I sat up and watched the body of the reptile float down the rapids in a murky red swirl of scales and flesh. Further down the river was a herd of hippos, eating the weeds and resting in the cool water from this humid air. I looked behind me to see the heart of the jungle.

"This is too much." Daniel cried. "I can take some hefty loads but this is...it's awful."

Samuel flustered screamed. " I'm sorry lads! How I was supposed to know where to go? I was just following the orders from Columbus and other sea farers."

"You clearly don't know where your going!" Daniel shouted. "You've drug us to our deaths in this jungle!"

Samuel angry pulled out his pistol and aimed it at Daniel's head and cocked it. His beard soaked from sweat. I shot up with Tim and pulled out my cutlass as Tim aimed his pistol at the Captain.

"Do it Captain. Go on." Daniel smirked.

Samuel eyed me aiming my blade at his neck, me pressing the blade against his skin. Tim had his pistol aimed at the captains head. Tim cocked the gun.

"I'm sorry sir, but we can't let you shoot our friend Dan here." Tim angrily bloated.

Samuel gulped still aiming the gun at Daniel. "I can still shoot him before you get your ring out on me."

"Aye, but will feed you to the pirañas instead." I smiled.

After saying that, I could see true fear in the captains old eyes. He slowly lowered his pistol. Tim kept it him at gun point. I grabbed the pistol from the captain and tossed it to the side in the grass. Daniel lowered his hands and walked over and picked up the gun.

"You lads really gonna shoot me." Samuel scoffed.

"No, but you will lead us out of this island. Back to the beach where we can build a fire and try to attract a ship to pick us up. We are done with this fairytale." I said.

"I could have you hanged for this in England." Samuel laughed.

"Aye, but will kill you first." Tim said.

Samuel gulped and we ushered him forward along the riverbank. Daniel shoved Samuel forward making him fall to the ground. "This is how you treat a captain?"

"You aimed a gun at my head sir." Daniel smirked. He picked up Samuel and pushed him forward to lead the way. Tim kept his pistol at his back as I kept my sword drawn. Daniel aimed the gun at the captain as we started to head along the riverbank. The tall green grass swayed in the hot air as we walked. As Samuel walked ahead of us, staying far from the rivers edge, he smirked loudly.

"The crew always backstabs the captain." He laughed in a raspy voice.

"Not true, but in this case yes." I said.

"What? You think aiming a pistol at my head was a smart move?" Daniel snickered at the old man.

"I was tired of your spit and scoff." He said.

"So you decided to end my life just because I didn't agree with you." Daniel said sternly.

The captain didn't answer. "Lads I-" suddenly a yellow spear hit into the grass next to Samuel's boots.

Samuel yelped backwards. I then heard a loud horn echo through the jungle and I looked behind to see a herd of black man with spears running at us, aiming bows and spears.

"Run!" I screamed.

We sprinted into the jungle as pushing past the tall palm leaves. I hacked the vines and thorns with my blade as we ran over dead leaves. Samuel was ahead of us all sprinting his old legs out. Tim turned around as he ran and fired his gun as it echoed with smoke. The bullet hit a tribal man in the head making him fall dead in a plume of blood. Spears and arrows whistled through the air hitting the ground and bark of the tree's next to me barely missing my body. Daniel fired his gun taking down two men in one shot. As Tim reloaded his gun, an arrow hit next to his feet, but he dodged it and fired the gun, the lead ball piercing the gut of a man making his belly squirt red. The tribals screamed and called after us in an unknown language. I ran through the vines and past stones deeper into the jungle. A spear ten feet long sailed after my spine. I rolled out of the way sideways as the spear zipped through the air past my body and jammed into the log. I gazed behind me as I kept running to see the endless horizon of black man. There were a hundred at least. My feet slapped the leaves, my heart thumped in my chest as if it was wanting too shoot out of my ribcage. My legs felt loose and tired, my body getting tired from running. The humid air sucked the breath out of me and stuck to my body like glue. Arrows spun by, almost clipping Daniel in the side. As Samuel trudged ahead, a arrow zipped by me and shot into his right leg. He screamed and stumbled to the ground. I ran and slide across the leaves to his aid. I gripped his arms and picked him up as Tim and Daniel fired the pistols only taking down a few of them. The arrow was stuck halfway into his leg and the sharp end was sticking out through his leg from his calves to his shin. Blood oozed out. Samuel's eyes flicked and rolled in his head, and his body was shivering. I heard the eerie call of a tribal man as I turned to get a stone club to my head and everything went to black.

My vision was blurry as I woke up. I looked down at my hands to see both of them were bonded in rope. I heard the beating of drums as I slowly looked up, my head throbbing and blood trickling down the side. I looked to my left to see Daniel and Tim on their knee's bonded in rope.

"What's happening?" I asked them.

Tim and Daniel just looked at me and true fear filled their faces. I looked away from them to see various straw huts laid about. The huts were a couple feet tall and came to a point at the top. Openings sat in the front of the huts. Huts dotted the jungle over growth, and black men walked around holding spears and bows. Face paints of blue, red, and yellow lined their faces and tattoos of unknown creatures painted on their bodies. The skin was so dark it was as if I was looking at midnight itself. There giant white eyes stared at us in confusion and intrigue.

Women that were shirtless and wore straw dresses walked around the encampment carrying pots full of water or food, as naked children ran around the place laughing. A few of the strong men, muscle bound, were standing next to a fire crackling away in a Bed of twigs and stones and a fat animal was being cooked over it. Samuel was in front of us, hands tied, his stringy hair in a mess, with two men holding onto each of his shoulders. A big black man walked over with a huge blade that curved at then end to Samuel. I gulped knowing we were going to be dead. I slowly without the tribals seeing, slipped the small knife I had under my belt. I began to slice away at the rope softly. The blade cut into the rope but it was tough to chop it as the angle I was sitting. My rope gave way finally, and I handed Tim the knife who cut himself free, then Daniel did the same. We still had our swords with us but our pistols were gone. The man with a big blade aimed it down on Samuels bare neck. He looked at us three.

"Run lads!" He cried as the blade hacked off his head. His head tumbled to the ground in a blood puddle. His headless body fell to the side. My heart stopped seeing our captain executed before my eyes.

"Run!" I screamed.

We all three shot up and began running out of the camp back into the jungle. As I ran I pulled out my sword. The men chased after us through the jungle throwing spears as they whistled by us again. This time the men were faster and caught up to us.

I turned around and slashed my sword hitting the edge of the spear deflecting it off to the left. I jabbed my sword into the black man's side making him fall dead. Daniel was in utter combat with two men as Tim was using his sword to attack the bow men.

I collided a sharp blade with his. The black man screamed in my face and stuck out his pink tongue crazily. His eyes were big and wide with black dark pupils. Face paint was covering his face and he was bald. He pushed me back. I stumbled to the ground to my knee's.

I raised my sword and dodge his right swipe. I rolled out of the way and cut at his calves making him fall backwards. I then stood up and stabbed him in the neck. He choked and died once I pulled the blade out.

I looked up to see an arrow sizzling towards my neck. I ducked under it hearing it zip by my head and rolled jamming my blade into a man. As Tim dodged a thrown spear, and Daniel killed a few men, we were outnumbered. Three against two hundred. We soon were overpowered and were forced to run deeper into the jungle. As I ran, trying to dodge the arrows flying by us, I tripped and fell down a small drop off. I rolled down the dead leaved hill smacking my side into a giant palm tree. I yelped in pain hearing my ribs crack.

I sat up gripping my side and felt my side throb. I gritted my teeth in pain as I slowly stood up and looked up from the ledge. I had lost the tribal men which was good but I had also lost Daniel and Tim.

"Tim?! Daniel?!" I cried up the ledge.

I didn't get an answer and fear rose inside me that they were killed by the tribe. I saw my blade on the ground covered in shiny blood. I picked it up and gripped my side.

"I gotta find a way out of here. I gotta find them." I said to myself.

I slowly hobbled with my blade in my right hand and my left keeping pressure on my ribs, trudged through the jungle. I pushed past tall giant leaves hacking them away with my sword, but the swiping from my blade was killing my side. I could feel my ribs crack under my arms movement. I groaned in pain as my feet shuffled through the leaves. As I sliced through the jungle, with my sword, the Eucalyptus leaves tumbling to the forest floor.   As I swiped through the next leaves, a tribal man, darker then a coffee bean, he swung his stone axe at me. I ducked it hearing it swish over my head, but I lost my blade in the process. My longsword skidded across the leaves as I hit the ground. Once hitting the ground I put my hands out to rolled to my side, my ribs poking the edge of my skin. I yelled in fear of the man about to strike me down and in pain of my broken ribs. He slung his stone axe towards my chest, but with all my strength I rolled out of the way his axe clamping down on the dirt. I kicked his ankle making him stumbled a bit. I crawled to my sword as fast as I could through the leaves, my ribs rubbing my side. I gripped the hilt but the man kicked me. I coughed and screamed in pain. I rolled over as the dark man covered in face paint and tribal tattoos was facing his axe blade to my heart. A necklace of animal bones and fingers surrounded his neck. My eyes stared into his with fear, forcing the stone to my body. I looked side to side and saw a big rock next to me. With all my might, I reached for it. My hand gripped it and I slung it over into the side of his head. His eyes rolled up for a second and a the rock thudded against his scalp. The man stumbled over. I gripped the golden hilt tightly bringing the sword round. As the man of the jungle regained his balance, he popped up ready to attack for another jab. Just before he was about to strike, I sliced my sword across his throat, and blood poured out of his neck like the cork of a champagne bottle bursting out. His warm blood splattered on my mouth and face. The taste of copper hit my tongue and I spit it quickly out. He gripped his throat suffocating on his own blood and toppled over to his side.

I sat up setting my sword to my side and held onto my side. My ribs burned at my side, poking out at the flesh. My side was black and blue, and bruised from the impact of the trunk. I gripped my golden hilt and used my body weight against the sword to lift myself up. I stabbed the blade into the dirt and lifted myself up. I drove it away, and peered at the neck slit black body to my right. He lay still, all naked except for a cloth that covered his private parts. I gazed up at the sky, the tree branches curling around blocking the sky as the sun shined through the wicked branches of these silent brown giants.

I used my bloody blade to hack away green tangly vines like serpents swirled together in a mass of thorns. The vines snapped away and I proceeded through the jungle limping. My hand against my left side as it stung and ached, my sword in my right, my eyes zoomed in and out, my heart steady, and breath heavy. My forehead felt hot, which it could be from the humid weather, but it was hotter like I was coming down with a fever. My movements were weaker and slower, my limbs felt weak. I stumbled to my knees yelling in pain and frustration. I coughed up some blood as it dripped down my lips like red rose petals falling off a stem. I spit the dark blood onto the dirt and looked up at the endless dense vegetation before me. I was lost, in pain and hurt, bleeding, ribs broke, and lost my friends and Captain Samuel was dead, beheaded before my eyes. His horrid image of his head toppling off his neck like a piece of silk being torn stung my mind with fear. As I focused on this terrible thought, I started to hear singing.

The voice was female. It reminded me of Brita's singing voice and at first I thought it was merrily me going crazy, and my mind fooling me. A cruel trick of the mind when one's brain starts to shut down in these barren lands.

I missed Brita so much and I longed for her touch on my body and the warm kiss upon my lips as if the world just broke into spring. I had my hands on the dirt, and listened to the sweet melody. I kept hearing the sweet music but this time I noticed it wasn't in my head but actually real. I looked up and could hear the running water in the distance. I quickly stood up and as fast as I could followed the voice. I limped through the jungle. The voice seemed to control my movements, like my mind wasn't my own and the entrancing tune swirled around my ears like nats. I couldn't help but be drawn to it and I started at a run. The pain didn't even bother my jolting ribs against my side as I sprinted through the forest. The deathly uncanny animals sounds of the jungle died down and all I could hear was the sweet humming of the voice. Finally, I fell through giant leaves into a wide open lagoon. What my eyes befell was beautiful, the most beautiful part of the jungle I had seen yet. I still heard the voice but didn't see anyone around. The wide open field was short thin grass of green that was across as if the grass had just been cut. Before me was a decent size pool of the bluest and clearest circle of water I had ever seen. Giant plants of leaves and tree's surrounded the outer edges of the lagoon, as yellow and blue and purple and pink and orange and red flowers dotted the grass. Big black boulders sat around the lagoon and the edge of the lagoon had black sand. A small waterfall fell between the cracks of the rocks. The voice still controlled me and I slowly walked over to the edge of the water. I peered over a black rock to see something my eyes couldn't believe. Bathing in the water, was what I thought was a naked woman humming to herself. She was beautiful, like actually beautiful. Her long brown hair extended down to half of her body. Her skin was milky white. Her breasts big and round like pearls. Her belly was flat. She had fat red lips and a small nose and green eyes. I scanned to under the shallow to see half of her lower body was a fish tail. Her silver orange tail swayed under the water. I was frozen in fear, amazement and shock. I rubbed my eyes to double check myself but she was still there. Samuel was right. She continued to sing entrancing my mind. The music danced around me happily. Suddenly the mermaid looked in my direction and we met eyes. I froze not moving, my sword still clutched in my hand.

She studied me for a minute with confusion. "Hello. I didn't know anyone was listening." She softly said under the waterfall.

I didn't respond.

"What are you doing here?" She asked me.

I finally was able to speak. "I uh, was stranded on this island. My ship had sunk and I got separated from my crew. I'm lost."

The mermaid looked around the lagoon and back at me. "You're not running. Why aren't you?"

She then looked at her tail and kicked it under the water, her silvery orange tail swayed under the blue. "I guess you can't see. My...fins and scales."

Suddenly a great fear came over me and I remembered what sirens can do to a man. I shot up and began taking off sprinting across the grass back into the jungle to hopefully try and find Tim and Daniel.

"Wait! Wait! Come back!" She called after me but I kept running.

She then began to sing. Suddenly I stopped running and turned around and walked back to the waters edge with no will of my own. Once I made it to the waters edge, she stopped singing.

"Come here. You can't leave my voice. You can't leave the water and you can't leave me. That's my gift to you, you must take it." She begged ushering me to come closer raising her and high in the water.

"Gift? What gift? What do I get in return?" I asked randomly. It was like I had no control over what I was saying.

"And in return, you can give yourself to me." She grinned a wide row of white teeth that shined in the sun.

"I don't think I want to. I-" but she cut me off.

"Come closer." She ushered with her arm for me to come in the water. "Yes, come here."

I tried to pull away but she sang again with that entrancing medley. I had no control over myself and stepped into the lagoon. It wasn't very deep to be honest, maybe only a few feet. The water was so crystal clear. I could make out the tiny pebbles and sand grains at the bottom. I slowly swam to her. I then was sucked underwater and could hear nothing but the dead sound of water running. It was like my body felt weightless. I struggled to swim but the mermaid grabbed me and lifted me up. I frantically kicked in the water trying to stay afloat and was afraid of her. Her tail swished under the current.

"Ugh stop." She complained as I thrashed. "Stop."

She put her hand on my chest. "It's okay." Her hand on my chest I suddenly felt calmer and safe like nothing bad was going to happen to me.

She kept her hand on my chest and then lifted my shirt over my head until I was shirtless. She grinned at my musclier body and scars from the battle and shipwreck from a month ago.

She looked deep into my eyes as if trying to take my soul with those green eyes. "Do you not like the water?"

The waterfall bounced off my head creating a nice calming cool stream down my spine. My injuries that I sustained seem to be subsiding in the water and my body felt warmer and more healed.

"No it's not that. I like the water actually." I said to her and now I somehow felt safer and calm around her.

"The lagoon is the most beautiful part of the jungle. It's like the heart of the island. Breathing out into the ocean." She smiled deeply into my eyes. My heart thumped loudly in my chest and for some reason I felt attracted to her. When she said heart it reminded me of what Samuel had told me about looking for the heart of the jungle.

The mermaid looked at my pants and boots. "I don't want to put you back on land."

"Uh why?" I asked.

"You might stay with me?" She pleaded.

"Stay with you?" I asked. "But I uh, can't swim like you do."

This shocked the mer-women. "You can't swim? But how? Everything is swim. The tree's swim in the breeze, and the birds swim in the wind. Then the snake swims across the earth. The dark clouds swim in the pouring rain. And my voice swims into your ears. Everything swims."

"But I'm not like you." I said.

She laughed softly. Her voice entranced me. "I don't mind if your not like me. You can still swim with me." She placed her hand on my chest and took a breath. "Oh your warm. The water can be so cold." She whispered.

"It is cold yes." I stuttered.

"I would like to have someone around me all the time. Would you come into the ocean with me?" She asked me with those alluring seaweed eyes.

"But I cannot breath underwater and I prefer land mostly." I pleaded but she frowned.

"No, I don't want to put you back on the beach. It's lonely out there. Down here with have each other. I'm not going to hurt you. I want you to swim with me. And we can pretend like were dancing, like-" the mermaid put on finger on her grinning lips, "I have legs and feet to walk on, like a woman you might love. If I could walk, would you love me if I could walk?"

I looked into her eyes and a feeling of love overwhelmed me. "I would." I said. "But it's okay that you can't."

She smiled widely. "I'd love you, even if you had nothing to stand on and nothing to swim with or nowhere to go. Are you scared?" She asked me.

I nodded fast. She put a finger up to my lips and shushed me quietly. "Don't feel like that. It's safe. We are safe, you and I. I've watched people like you for so long."

"You've watched us?" I asked.

"Sailors who love the sea and women in pretty dresses who wished they didn't. And those small human children, who can only go so far into the water, before mother calls them back. I think of it like me, who can only go so far until the waves pull me back in. I know there's no place for me on land, I know that now. But...there's a place here for you." She raised her arm across the lagoon as if showing me for the first time.

"Really?" I asked.

"There is." She nodded. "I see those like you enter the water. So many times, but they don't stay. So maybe I can help."

"Help how?" I asked.

"I feel like you must want it so much, but you always return to the soil. Every time. Its like you choose to make me jealous of your walking and running. You do that to hurt me it seems." She pouted.

"What? No of course not! Not to hurt you!" I yelled in sadness.

"You venture into my world, you tease me, for being unable to experience yours. I can only be still and watchful. It's not fair, not at all." She frowned.

I put my hand to her cheek looking into those sad eyes of hers. She looked up at me. "Do you still love me?"

"Of course I do." I smiled.

"I'm starting to feel like you don't. Starting to feel like your lying to me. Are you lying to me?" She frowned.

"What? No I'm not lying!" I shouted.

"Will you stop lying if I bring you into the ocean?" She asked me.

"Yes." I said.

"Will you love me if I bring you into the water with me?" She begged.

"Yes." I said.

"You can come down, you can come underwater. Come." She grabbed my head and we both sank beneath the waves.

My eyes were blurry but I could still see clearly the clear face of the beautiful mermaid.I couldn't believe they were real and this one was so nice to me.

Then I realized my lungs were breaking and I shot up gasping for air. As I did this, the mermaid looked at me puzzled.

"Why are you fighting me? I want you to come out to sea with me. So we can be together. I can help you. I can give you to the water. Just like all your kind wants. You don't have to go back, just come down with me." This time saying it more forceful.

She placed her soft delicate hands on my shoulders and drove me back underwater.

As the crushing depth of the water surrounded me, my body began to feel trapped, I couldn't move, and my limbs grew weary. My heart started to beat faster at the rate I wasn't used too. My whole body seemed to jolt. My ears rang and popped under the pressure of the waterfall. I looked at the mermaid before me,, her silver tail sloshing under the water creating small bubbles and her emerald eyes staring into mine with lust.

I shot up spitting up water, my lungs feeling tired.

"Why? Why won't you come under with me?" She pleaded sadly.

"Uh cause I can't breath." I said.

"Do you hate me so much?" She cried a tear running down her cheek.

"No I don't hate you!" I cried out.

"Why do you continue to tease me? Why would you make me fall in love with you and then leave me? Always back to your land." She wailed.

"I'm not leaving you." I said assuringly.

"No! No more. I don't want to be like those ladies in the pretty dresses. Watching there jolly sailor bold disappear forever. I must have you. I MUST! I MUST!" She screamed.

The mermaid shoved me back underwater but this time she didn't let me go. She kept me under and I tried to swim up to the surface, but my arms and legs wouldn't work. My lungs started to break under the stream. My eyes started to become a cloud of black mist. I looked at the swirly face of the beautiful mermaid before my eyes and instead saw a creature of horror. Her eyes were sharper and clean, and her row of teeth we jagged sharp spears. She grinned a wide creepy grin under the water. Her tail turned into sharp scales and I could her muffled laugh under the water. She gripped my shoulder holding me down tightly until I couldn't breath anymore. My heart was thumping so loud in my chest. I thrashed as hard as I could but it was no use. Her fangs opened wide as she darted towards my neck. I screamed under water but just before the bite, my vision turned into a mixture of bubbles and swirl. My body flew up out of the lagoon, and plopped onto my back on the grass. As I landed on the grass, the mermaid jumped out trying too grab me but a shot rang out and hit her tail. She wailed in pain and flopped onto the land and couldn't move cursing in an unknown tongue. Her silver tail at the end oozed blood. She screeched as Daniel dragged me out away from the water, Tim to my right aiming a steaming pistol at the creature. Daniel lifted me up and slapped me straight across the face.

"What in gods name were you doing?!" He shouted.

"I-" I couldn't speak I was still in shock.

"Henry get ahold! What is that?" Tim shouted.

I backed up and looked at the hurt mermaid. Blood trickled down the silver tail onto the grass. "Hello sailors. Why don't you come into my water so I can eat you!" She laughed.

"There real?" Daniel exclaimed in shock.

"Aye!" I yelled.

"Henry what were you doing under the water? We came running over and saw you just sitting underwater with her. If it wasn't for Daniel, you would have drowned." Tim yelled in astonishment.

"I don't know. What happened to you two?" I asked.

"We lost you lad. We escaped the tribe but got utterly lost as well. We tried searching for you until we stumbled into this lagoon opening. Then we saw you dip under water with a woman. Well a demon fish." Daniel scowled at the hurt creature.

She laid on her side, her tail steaming in the sun and scales shining bright."Oh, come my love to me." She started to sing but Daniel kicked grass into her face.

"Quiet you wretch!" He screamed.

"What happened?" Tim asked.

"I don't know. I hurt my side and then started to hear her sing. I followed her voice and it was like I had no control over my body. I just followed her command. Then she lured me into the water and we talked and she tricked me and tried to kill me." I scowled at her.

She smirked. "I was hungry." She pouted out.

"What are you?" I asked.

"A creature of many things. Myths to you sailors." She giggled in a pitted voice.

"Glad your alright mate. Now what are we going to do with her? Samuel was right lads! He was right! I feel awful that I disregarded his word." Daniel frowned. "Now's he dead."

I clapped his shoulder. "We did too. It's good, we didn't know. Now, how are we going to get her caged?"

"Caged?" She asked.

"Aye, we are going to cage you and take you back to England to collect the prize." Tim smiled at the glory that awaited us.

"Absurd!" She shouted in worry.

"Aye tis is but we will keep you alive fish lady." Daniel smirked. "You have lured our kind to their deaths for centuries you demon fish women! How could you do a such a thing?"

"Because the sea is our place. Not a place for a man." She smiled, her fangs gone and she put back on the face of a "innocent" women.

"Sea is for men." Tim said.

The mermaids scales began to burn and shin in the sun as she cried in pain.

"Please, I need the water! My scales are peeling! Help!"

I rolled my eyes and walked over and scooped up the cool water with my hands. I dumped it on her silver tail and the blood washed away and her scales stopped burning for a minute.

"You can't leave the water?" I asked.

"No, only for a time. That's why I never belong on land." She frowned. "Now sailors how do you plan to trap me."

"I have a idea." Daniel grinned widely.

Within forty five minutes, we constructed a case of water for the mermaid to be put into. We measured her size and estimated how long we needed to make the casing. From there, we cut down some bamboo stalks and bent them into a square rim. We collected sand and used Daniel's matches to melt it down and heat and melt into wet glass. We then dried the glass in cool water, and place a glass cage around the boxy bamboo holders. We constructed a glass lid above that. We then picked up the women fish which was heavier than the crates and struggled to drop her in to the caging. She splashed into the water and now we could see her in the case and removed the lid of the trap.

"This is how you treat a women?" She asked us all.

"Your not a women." I scowled at her.

She frowned and her eyes dripped tears but my heart was ice cold for this creature after her trying to kill me. After we finished we walked the lagoon circumference and at the glaring sun and figured out we were only a few miles South of the beach shore just by looking at the clouds and sun and the time of day. We assumed it was around 2:30. The sun beamed down on our heads creating the humid air.

"Lads we are four lengths out from the sand. We have to carry the casing through the jungle, but let's stay close to the riverbank for it will spill into the ocean I'm sure." Daniel said.

"Well how do we know the river won't just follow into another river?" Tim asked.

Daniel gave him a confused look. "What?"

"You know, the brown water could flow into a bigger river deeper into the jungle." Tim noted.

"True." I said thinking and then I looked up high into the sky. "We seem to be 34 nautical off so if we follow the tree line tops North-West to the approximate latitude of 56 and 78 we should make it to the beach before nightfall."

"Just follow-" The mermaid tried to speak but Daniel hushed her.

"Quiet lady of the ocean I'm thinking!" He shouted annoyed.

"I'm trying to help you." The fish creature said.

"Help us how?" I asked.

"I told you, that the lagoon is the heart of the jungle. It flows to the ocean. Just follow its stream." The fish women told us through the glass floating ever so slightly. She rested her arms over the glass rim, keeping them folded over each other and resting her head on her arms. Her long soft brown hair flowed into the glass cage of water. Her tail was curled to the side.

"What stream?" Tim questioned.

"That stream." The mermaid said pointing to the gorgeous blue stream cutting from the lagoon pool into the jungle.

"How did we not see that?" I whispered.

Daniel shrugged. "Come on, let's get to the beach."

149

Within a few hours of constant trudging through the jungle carrying the heavy glass case with a mermaid in it, we struggled to keep it up. It was bulky and heavy and we tossed and turned down various hills and rocks making the mermaid spin and slosh in the water. We had to avoid giant insects and snakes but within a sunset time, we made it back to the red sandy beach.

We had set the water cage down on the beach, and Daniel constructed a fire with stones and matches and dead leaves. The fire cracked warm as the air turned from hot to cold by the ocean. The sun dipped below the horizon in a purple glare and the sky turned black and the white stars twinkled above. The fire was the only light and the sounds of the jungle behind us, was echoed out by the crashing of waves. We had found some left over food in the stranded crates and I found a old guitar. It was a little damaged from the wreck but it strummed just fine. We ate by the fire quietly, and the fire created a big cloud of grey smoke high into the night sky.

The mermaid watched us eat with such intent, I swear she looked like she had never seen a man eat before.

Daniel tossed a few branches into the fire as the bark burned. "That should hopefully send a signal for a passing ship to see."

Tim was laying on his back looking up at the stars as Daniel was eating the remaining dried meat. I strummed the guitar quietly. The tune echoed through the beach softly. The mermaid watched me mostly, since I was the one she interacted with the most before. As I played the instrument Daniel watched me.

"Since when could you play?" He asked tossing some meat between his teeth.

"Brita taught me." I said.

Daniel laughed. "Oi, a women teaching a man of such things. Absurd right Tim me boy?"

Tim propped up on one elbow in the sand. "I suppose."

Daniel laughed and looked at me but I kept a serious look on my face and didn't enjoy the comment he had made. Daniel frowned in the firelight.

"Sorry my lad. Just never really had a real women like you have gotten back in Norway." Dan sadly muttered.

150

I continued to strum the music quietly. "So what can you play? Any ballads?" Daniel asked me.

"Aye. I can play a few she taught and sang to me. There's one that is my favorite. It's called the DornishMan's wife. Heard of it?" I asked.

They both shook their heads. I smiled slightly. "Well, I shall play it for ye." I closed my eyes beside the fire in the night, and began to strum the guitar. When Brita would play this song with me she would play the piano I had gotten for her for Christmas. The piano played first. I closed my eyes and could utterly hear the piano keys from her fingers hitting them. Then I began to strum the instrument. As my fingers picked the strings I smiled up into the sky as the mermaid watched with lust and curiousness.

I strummed with such power and remember the nodes and notes she had taught me to strum for this ballad. My voice rang out over the ocean and hit everyones ears with delight. Daniel and Tim sat still by the fire, shocked as ever to hear my voice. A wide grin formed on the edge of both of their grins. The mermaid watched through the watery glass, her head propped up over the edge listening and she had her eyes closed and a thin smile on her face. My voice mixed with the fire flicker.

Once the lyrics passed Daniel and Tim joined in at the end. Tim clapped loudly to the beat. Tim stood up and did a rig and jig around the fire laughing. Once I finished strumming and singing Daniel and Tim clapped loudly.

"Oi, my lad! You're a singer at the heart!" Tim laughed running up to me and tackling me to the sand.

Daniel ruffled my long brown hair. "Looks like the lassie taught you well! A good girl!"

"She's amazing." I smiled to myself. "I hope we can make it back to Norway so I can see her."

"Aye lad! We will! Will get a ship to take us there, and will drink dark rum and sing shanties in the town! You'll get your lassie and me and young Tim will find us some women to tend to us!" Daniel laughed taking a swig of the dirty watery rum that was left from the crate.

Daniel tossed me the bottle and I took a nasty swig of the burning liquid. Tim drank next raising his glass high in the firelight.

"To us lads! For surviving hell and taking it down to the depths!" He cried.

"Aye mates!" I laughed happily.

"I sure hope this smoke heathers to the ship passing." Daniel said.

I gazed up at the tall grey plume in the inky black sky. "Aye it'll hold."

"We need to track down Baggins." Tim snarled.

"In due time lad. In due time he will have his." Daniel said.

Later that night, Tim and Daniel passed out drunk by the fire snoring away. I sat by the fire still awake. I couldn't sleep. I was carving a sharp small spear from a twig with my knife to keep my mind off such horrid things that I have experienced. I was wanting to keep my hopes high in the heavens.

I couldn't believe the legendary women of the sea was in a glass case behind me from the fire. I would have never believed such things, but now I don't know what to believe. I started to question my believe in God, not really thinking if there was a man in the sky.

Maybe man was meant to roam the earth to just glaze the surface while some were meant to discover such discoveries unknown to man and not meant to be seen.

As I fiddled with the stick, I heard the movement of water. "Sailor." The mermaid called over to me.

I glanced over my shoulder at the sea creature in the case. "What?" I asked her.

"Come heather over." She pleaded.

I scoffed. "So you can try to kill me again?"

"No." She shook her head. "Just to speak."

I stopped messing with the twig and sat in the red sand for a minute. Talking to this creature intrigued me to know her secrets and why she did what she does. I threw the twig in the fire and walked over shaking the sand off my ass. I plopped down next to the case as the mermaid sat up over the rim next to me.

"Speak of what?" I asked.

"You sang earlier." She mentioned.

"Aye." I said looking at my knife silver in the moonlight.

"You sang the song with such passion. Why?" She asked me.

This surprised me, a creature of such origin asking such a question. "It meant something to me. My lover, she's back in Norway, taught me it and we sang it together. It makes me think her."

"Think of her?" The creature asked me.

"Aye. I think of her often. I love her." I grinned to myself.

"But you don't love me?" She scoffed.

"You tricked me, making me think I loved you." I said.

"Well I've never felt real love. What's it like?" She asked me.

I glanced up at her. My long hair hung down my shoulders. My scruff thicker in the firelight. "It's like um...it's like...a feeling you get. Your heart beats fast, your head topples in joy and excitement when you see or think of the person you love so grand. Your body shakes with a sensation of joy and love together. It's something a human feels when they see beauty in another."

The mermaid looked at me puzzled. "Is love dangerous?"

"It can be. It hurts sometimes." I said.

"Is Norway far?" The mermaid asked.

"Oh yes! Miles down the sea." I frowned.

"Oh, are you going back to her?" She asked me.

"I hope so. I don't think I will though. After what we have been through." I frowned.

"And what is that?" The beautiful creature wondered.

"What is what?" I asked looking into her eyes. When I looked into hers I, for a second felt like I was talking to another human.

"What you have gone through?" She wondered. "What was your mission?"
I frowned to myself. I looked at the creature as she stared at me with interest.
"I was a sailor aboard a ship called the Deltarone. Now she's sunk beneath
waves out there." I pointed my knife out to the blue. "We hit a storm. She
went under. Lost the whole crew to the waters and sharks. We were delivering
supplies to various countries around Europe and along the African Coast
from England. In return we would get coin. We ran into complications such
as a giant squid attacking our ship, a battle, and more. Our captain is dead in
the jungle and now were hopefully going to get off this rock."
The mermaid tried to understand this peril but it seemed to confuse her. "I'm
deeply sorry for you."
"Your sorry?" I asked shocked.
"Yes. That seems difficult to experience." The mermaid frowned at me and
for some reason I felt it actually seemed genuine.
"It's alright." I smiled slightly to myself.
We sat there in silence for a few minute listening to the crackling of the fire.
The mermaid sloshed in the water.
"What's your name sailor?" She asked me.
"Henry Heartstone." I said. "Do you have a name or are you the esteemed
fish lady?"
"I have a name. My mother called me Viviane." She smiled at me.
"Viviane?" I asked.
"Yes that was the name given to me at birth." Viviane told me.
"Where is your mother now?" I curiously wanted to know.
"She's dead. Killed by your kind I'm afraid." She sorely gritted her teeth.
"How did our kind kill her?" I questioned.
"They ran her over with their ship without even knowing." Viviane sighed.
"Well that wasn't their fault then, they had no idea." I said.
"I suppose so, but your kind are always drinking, enjoying the air, and
women, and always seem so happy. How can you be happy everyday?" Vivane
asked.

154

"We are not happy most of the time. Look at me, I'm stranded on a island off the coast, and been through hell and back within three months. Life isn't always great like you see it." I shrugged.

"Huh. It isn't great? Why? What's not great about it?" Vivane asked with such interest leaning forward almost falling over the edge of the glass cage.

"We have so many things to obey in society. Money, laws, taxes, royalty ,the king and queen. We lose loved ones through out life to the black crow. Life isn't always fair Vivian." I then sat there realizing something. I was actually enjoying teaching her about our lives.

"What's great about it?" She wondered.

"Well, we have rum and ale, delicious foods to eat, falling love with a lassie, exploring and traveling the world, money, a nice cottage, children of your own and watching them grow." I said.

"I see. Why do you sailors like the sea so much?" The mermaid asked me.

"There something about it that's alluring to me. Like its calming. With the helm under my hand, the waves churning under her hull, the crew singing the shanties and jigging on board, drinking ale to the heavens, the thrill of the unknown of what you'll encounter on the vast blue, it's as if you'r the only group of sailors out there and the world is in your hands to explore." I smiled.

"That's beautiful." She smiled.

"I have a question." I said.

"Yes?" Vivane asked.

"Why do you kill sailors at sea? Why do you lure them to their deaths?" I asked.

The mermaid froze for a minute and it looked like I asked to of a personal question to such a mythical being. She traced her finger on the rim of the edge of the glass.

"I was told by my mother that all men are bad. All they care about is having the women's body and not the person. You are careless, drunk, lazy, and only care what you want and take no consideration of the consequences you inflict on others. I was told to stay away from you, and to lure them to drown you. All of my kind is taught to stay hidden and lure to rid the world of sailors. But your kind interest me so. And I'm realizing that your not as bad as my mother made you out to be."

I actually smiled back at her making the mermaid smile. "Thanks. Your not as bad yourself." I said.

"Where are you from again?" She asked. "When were you born?"

"I was born in London, England in 1652." I said.

"Is it scary leaving England to these uncharted waters?" Vivane curiously asked.

"Aye. It is. But we sailors don't show fear because it is a sign of disrespect." I said.

"That's ridiculous for one to not show fear. I'm sure everyone feels fear." The mermaid said.

"Yes they do but people don't like to think they do." I said.

"What is it like being on one of those wooden houses?" She asked.

"Wooden houses?" I asked. "You mean a ship?"

"That's what that's called?" She laughed.

"Aye a ship, a water vessel of a sorts." I smiled at her curiousness.

"What's it like?" She asked.

"It's difficult most of the time but also amazing. Usually there is a captain who is the head of the crew, which I am part of the crew, and these two lovely lads asleep are too and my closest buds. The captain is the leader of a sorts. The crew follows his orders and cleans the ship and stocks its supplies and prepare for battle." I told her.

Her eyes danced with wonder. "Why do you follow his orders?"

"Because its law." I said.

"What's law?" She asked.

"A commitment you have to obey in society." I smiled.

"Being on a ship sounds magical." She smiled.

"Aye, and if we can get a ship to see us, you'll get to be on one." I smiled.

She smiled widely with a look of child like wonder. I smirked and stood up shaking the sand off me. "I'm heading to rest, you should too."

I tossed her a piece of bread and she caught it and ate it smiling to the taste of this new starch to her mouth. I laughed and walk closer to the fire. Before I sat down she reached her hand out.

"May I get closer to the fire? Please? It's cold." She pleaded.

I froze for a second but then nodded. I walked over and dragged the glass case closer to the fire next to me as the fire filled her with warmth. I plopped onto the red sand and laid on my back facing the stars. I pointed at the stars.

"You know many stars?" I asked her.

"My mother told me stories from the ocean floor." She smiled.

"Magical aren't they?" I asked.

"Yes." She grinned. She then paused for a minute. "I am sorry for....trying to kill you."

I looked up at her to see a true look of regret on her face. I smiled. "It's alright Viviane. Goodnight."

I closed my eyes and drifted off to the sound of the fire crackling in the night.

'

Madagascar
The Next Morning

"Henry get up! Ship approaching the shore!" Tim slapped my face waking me up and resulting in me punching him square in the face.

Tim flopped backwards gripping his nose. "Shit Henry."

"You slapped me." I muttered groggily.

I sat up and saw a wooden ship sailing into shore. The wooden ship was the same size as the Deltarone. It wooden hull and sides were painted bright white and blue. Yellow streaks lined down her sides. The blue sails flushed in the wind with a giant deck with thousands of green jacketed armed men plowed towards the shore. I watched as the hatches dropped on the side of the right ship, it steered right starboard. Canons of black popped out of the holes and within a few seconds fired at us.

"Canon fire!" Daniel yelled.

We hit the sand as the balls sailed over us with a giant crack into the jungle. Sand flew up in a wave over our heads. Viviane was frantically trying to stay safe in the glass but if a canon ball took it out she'd be done.

I spit the sand out of my mouth and looked up to see the ship weigh anchor. Rowboats were dropped to the water and a burly man jumped down into the boat. The burly man and twelve other crew men rowed to the red sand. Within a few minutes, the rowboat scraped up onto the wet sand. The burly man hopped over the edge and trotted up the sand, as his crew members hauled the boat to still. The giant man had a stock of red curly hair on his head and a bushy red beard across his face. He wore a kilt, and a green cloak. He carried a giant scabbard with him.

"Morning lads." He smiled.

We all stared up at Colin Baggins in shock. We were still in shock from the canon fire.

"You aren't talking? All you boys did was talk at that tavern in Dublin." He laughed.

We slowly stood up shaking the sand off. "I wouldn't reach for your swords." Colin aimed his a pistol at me.

"How did you find us?" I asked.

"It was simple lads. I had the German's sink your ship to the deep just off the coast of Madagascar. I knew if you some of you were lucky enough to survive, which you clearly were, three of ya, then it was just a matter of time before I find you. I also knew Samuel was looking for a mermaid, just off this coast and I couldn't let him claim that glory all himself." He grinned. "Where's Samuel?"

"He's dead." Tim said.

"Oh." Baggins pouted. "Tragic."

"Why did you attack our ship when we battered with you in good faith back in Dublin?" Daniel spat out.

Colin laughed a hearty laugh. "That coin and supplies belonged to me. All the ships that pass through the Irish seas are mine to claim. Now." Colin pulled out a scroll of paper from his coat. He unrolled it carefully. "You gents are to be taken to Denmark, to be sold as English pirates to the Dutch to work for em. Your lucky day! In order of the King of Denmark!"

"What? How-" I tried to speak but he punched me in the gut sending me into the sand coughing.

Daniel ran at him but Colin aimed his pistol at Daniel. "I would stop if I were you. Now please obey me or you'll be shot and I don't want to clean up blood off these nice beaches."

I sat up coughing my gut punched through. Then Colin noticed the mermaid. His eyes widened with amazement. He lowered his pistol and slowly walked over to the glass casing. Vivane glared at him in fury.

"Why do you hurt them?" She frowned.

"My god it cannot be." He said. "A beautiful mythical creature of the deep."

"Don't touch her!" I shouted.

Baggins looked at me laughing. "Shut up you pirate. Bind em, and take this creature to the ship so I can study her."

Within a hour we were bonded with hard ropes, tossed in the rowboat, brought to the ship, and thrown onto the deck as Vivane was brought to the lower deck for studying.

"It'll be okay!" I assured her worried face as the glass case descended.

Colin picked me up and opened a hatch on the upper deck. He tossed Daniel and Tim inside. "You care for the creature? How lovely. Now you can rot in this cell until we get to Denmark pirate!"

He kicked me in the side, and pushed me backwards and I fell into the hatch with Daniel and Tim and two crew men shackled our feet and hands with iron. They took the lock key, and climbed out, closing the hatch leaving us three in complete darkness with little light.

On the route to Denmark
January 1680

We spent 7 months inside that hatch. 7 months. Over the months off being
stuck down in that hole we were only allowed food and water once a day.
They only time we were brought out of the darkness was to be washed and to
wash the flitch of shit, piss, and pus in the hatch from us. I knew Viviane was
safe in her glass case, but she was a display to the crew always eyeing her like
she was some demon. She was mythical and strange but she had emotions just
like any of us and was still part human. That bastard Colin Baggins
sometimes brought us up from the hatch to laugh in our faces and spill beer
on our faces as humility to the crew as the crew echoed their jars.
Rats had become our friends down in this shit hole as the irons rubbed our
ankles and wrists to numb scabs. The trip to Denmark was taking longer than
excepted. Although, being on this ship for 7 months us three have memorized
such a ship that we knew where everything was stashed.
Now it was night the moonlight shown through the cracks of the wood. We
had constructed a small key from reminding chains that laid about the floor in
the dark. I knew it was midnight and most of the crew was resting.
"Alright lads, let's do this." I smiled.
I stuck the key in the iron and it clicked free. Daniel and Tim did the same.
We kicked the chains away. We climbed up the creaky ladder and I unlocked
the hatch. I slowly opened it and peered over the rim. No crew mates were
around except for one single watchmen at the edge of the rim, looking out
over the sea to my left. We slipped up from the hatch and closed the lid as
quietly as possible. The sails swayed in the silent night breeze as glowing
lanterns dotted the masts. I moved my fingers in a formation to take out the
sailor. Daniel crouched walked to the sailor and broke his neck hearing the
snap. The sailor fell silent and Daniel took his sword. I joined Daniel with
Tim.

"Okay. Where are the muskets?" Tim asked.

"Down below." Daniel whispered.

"Okay, me and Tim will grab the muskets. Daniel grab lantern and will set her ablaze. The will free the mermaid and make for the rowboats." I smiled. We all nodded and broke off. Daniel fetched a lantern as me and Tim tip toed down the deck. We passed by the sailors snoring away in their hammocks, stepping like a mouse. We didn't wake a soul. Me and Tim gripped two muskets, with powder and ball and took the other with us. We went up the deck and threw the rest of the guns overboard watching them sink into the sea. The brown stocks disappeared beneath the foam. We loaded the muskets stuffing the lead ball deep within the shaft. I poured in the powered and lit the flaming match against the side and a small flame like a tiny heart lit the rope fuse.

Daniel had spilled oil all under the decks from the barrels.

"Let's set her ablaze!" Daniel shouted a whisper.

He lit a match and dropped it on the oil down below deck by the hammocks. The flame caught a spread down the line catching the sleeping sailors and barrels and rope on fire. We hurried up the wooden steps and waited for the sailors to climb out. The ship burned as the flame scorched across the entire ship engulfing her in orange and yellow in the night. The flame bounced and skipped shooting up the ropes of the mainmast and the timbers creaked to black wood. Pieces of the ship began to fall off and burn in crumbles of gray ash.

Soon, a cloud of smoke escape from under the deck, we could hear the panicked screams of the sailors below. They screamed in pain of being burned alive. We then heard the clamp of boots running up the steps, and we aimed our guns at the hole.

A engulfed sailor was the first out, we didn't fire and instead watched him claw at his face in agony as the flames peeled off his flesh into bloody sizzling drops on the deck. His eyes melted down out of his sockets and he toppled over the edge of the burning ship into the water with a splash. The next man was not on fire but he had severe burns across his neck and face. We shot him down where he stood, in his own blood. One after the other we loaded and fired popping off flaming pistol and musket fire shooting down the fire catches mates as they died in a scream of pain into the fires of hell that were ahead of them.

Finally, Baggins broke from his cabin with a long curvy blade. It glimmered in the ember glow of his burning ship. He was bewildered by his sailors laying in a puddle of burnt black flesh on the deck and running around screaming. He then realized the whole ship was on fire, and eyed us three standing below the deck.

"Henry!" He shouted jumping down in his night gown of white.

His boots smacked on the ashy deck as the blue sails ripped and blundered down into the cooling night water. The main mast creaked and groaned. The mast snapped in two and toppled down with a loud scream of groaning wood into the ocean with a white splash.

"You bastards!" He screamed looking around for any spare crew men. "Kill them you drabs!"

The remaining crew had grabbed a few pistols that were there own keepers.

"You'll pay for what you did." I grinned in the fire.

I leaped forward clinging swords with Baggins locking our eyes together. The swords clashed in the night creating sparks of red. He swung to my left and I rolled but I almost rolled into the flames just stopping myself in time and collided iron with the man again.

"Tim! Daniel to the boats! Cut em loose! I'll fetch Viviane!" I cried over the steel.

Daniel and Tim nodded and rushed over "Aye!" Tim shouted.

As they ran Colin noticed as them. He kicked me in the side and threw me over a blockade of fire. I landed with a hard thud and looked to my left at the rowboats. Baggins cocked his pistol and fired a bullet. It sailed through the air.

"Daniel! Tim! Bullet fire!" I shouted after them but I watched as the bullet hit a gunpowder barrel beside them.

The barrel exploded into a flame and they both sailed back. The blast even knocked me a few feet and half of the ship exploded into the water as it churned in the waves. Tim flew backwards and hit straight into my gut. We rolled a few feet back as I noticed Tim's arms were both ripped off from the blast. His bloody nubs sprayed blood onto the deck and his face was turning increasingly blue fast. He looked at me with shock, he opened his mouth trying to speak but utterly collapsed dead at my feet armless. My heart sank beneath my stomach. I peered at Daniel who was crawling over to me, sever burn marks on his skin burning red. He heaved in pain as he sat up, Colin walking over with his blade.

"Tim! The young boy! You fucker!" Daniel reached for his fallen pistol. He gripped it and cocked it. He fired a shot but the shot sailed just by the Captain grazing his side and he stumbled. Baggins laughed as blood oozed from his ribs.

"Nice shot." He said on his knees.

All of the crew were burned alive, and the ship was almost collapsing under the depths. The flames burned quickly, scorching close to my face as my body began increasingly hotter.

"Lad free Viviane now!" Daniel smiled and ran up to Baggins.

Baggins laughed and tried to raise his pistol to Daniel for another fire but Daniel kicked the pistol to the fire. Daniel picked Colin up in his arms, and pulled a knife out from his pocket and shoved it deep into the gut of the captain. Blood poured out of his mouth, spilling onto his lips. It mixed with the color of the flame and his kidneys plopped out. Daniel twisted the knife in and out inside Colin's gut making me whale in pain. Daniel's big musclier arms squeezed the man tight over the fire as it spurrier across the deck. I knew the ship was about to implode and crush us to Davy Jones locker. His blue veins throbbed in the fire light on his skin.

Baggins pulled a sword out. "You're all coming to Hell with me."

He stabbed the sword clean through Daniel's chest. It shot out his back and Daniel coughed out blood.   His eyes shimmered blue in the fire. Baggins laughed over the fire.

"No!" I screamed feeling tears run down my cheeks. My heart sank and froze seeing this before me.

Daniel eyed me straight into mine, and smiled the widest grin. "Aye lad! I may be greeting death but soon will meet in the heavens Henry me boy! Will drink rum and dine with passed kings and queens, and live like men!"

Daniel heaved upward and plummeted into the fire burning to a crisp killing Colin with him. Tears ran down my face as the ship began to sink into the waves. Flames surrounded me almost hitting my boots and my skin was sweating from the heat. I knew within ten minutes I would be burned flesh. I looked up into the stars wishing I could talk to Brita one last time.

Then I remembered the note she gave. I quickly reached inside my coat pocket and pulled out the piece of folded paper. I carefully unfolded the art, as ash flurried through the air, and smoke filled my lungs and wood fell. The paper was long, and black ink was down the page. At the top was her signature in pretty letters.

I read the message under the heat. "My love, I wish you luck on the rest of your voyage and hope you make it home to me safely. Know that I miss you, and I love you so much. I always will. I wrote you this poem just for you. If you ever are scared, or feel like you need me, you can read this and know I always will be waiting for your return and I will always love you. Read it, and imagine me singing it to you as I strum my lute as if I was by your side in the bed cuddled up by your side my darling. All the best my love, Brita.

I swallowed the tears as I looked down to the poem. I began to read it and imagine her voice and lute in my head drowning out the sounds of the burning ship around.

Upon one summer's morning
I carefully did stray
Down by the Walls of Wapping
Where I spied a sailor gay

Conversing with the young lass
Who seemed to be in pain
Saying, William when you go
I fear you'll never return again

His eyes so soft and tender
All her tears he wiped away
Saying Young lass don't you worry
For I'll come again one day

With all that she could muster
Her heart still torn in two
With these words she left her lover
As she promised to be true

My hearts been struck by Cupid
I disdain all glittering gold
There is nothing can console me
But my sailor

May fortune try to claim me,
I will never give wealth a thought
For my true love holds my longing
My love can not be bought

If war or pain or suffering,
Take hold of all I know,
I will still remain yours only,
Young or ill or old.

Remember me with fondness,

As the days grow long and cold.
I will always be here waiting,
With candle light a glow.

Good-bye my dear sweet sailor,
I can speak with you no more,
For I fear my heart a trembling,
Will not survive 'till morn.

And as she turned to leave him,
His hand did hold her still,
For he could not bear to leave her there,
So heart-broken until,

His arms around her tightly,
As he whispered in her ear,
With these words he left her softly,
His love true and sincere.

My dearest sweet Maria,
All the pain I cannot tell,
But my heart will stay here with you,
And with you always dwell.

No fortune, fame or sunrise,
Could e're with you compare!
There is nothing can betake me,
My sweetest maiden fair.

I'll watch the waves a rising,
And I'll count them one by one.
For I know these waves again one day,

I'll sail to take me home.

My dearest, sweet Maria,
I do wish that I could stay.
But we both know that a sailor's life,
Must ever be this way.

His hair dark as the midnight,
His eyes as black as coal,
With their last kiss they spoke softly,
Of unending love untold.

Her hair like burning embers,
Beauty rivaling the sun,
This is how he would remember her,
Until his journey home.

Remember that I love you,
Though worlds we be apart.
All I am will be yours ever,
From morning light thru dark.

My hearts been struck by Cupid,
I disdain all glittering gold,
There is nothing can console me,
But my sailor

Through perils, rain, and sunrise,
I'd have you this to know.
All my thoughts and prayers are with you,
Wherever you may go.

I will ne'er forget your promise,
One day to return home.

Once I finished reading it my heart thumped loudly for her. I looked up into
the white stars and saw them alined. "I love you Brita my singer." I said to
myself.

I then remembered Viviane and rushed up the deck dodging flames as the
ocean water poured over the sides to the deep. I hurried to the captains den,
and saw the glass case with Viviane frightened as ever. I punched through the
locked glass lid cutting my hand up. As blood ran down it I scooped her up
and picked her up, her silver tail flopping over my arms. I ran back outside
and looked to the see the entire ship was in flame. In a minute me and her
would be burned alive. I looked into her frightened eyes.

"I'm sorry." I frowned. "That we are going to die. I tried to save you."

She put a finger to my lip. The heat closed in. "It's alright. But, I can save
you and me."

"How can you?" I asked.

"Since you didn't kill me after I tried to kill you, I feel like I should offer my
help for your sweet grace." The mermaid smiled at me.

"What are you going to do?" I asked.

"Just trust me. Can you?" She asked me.

I looked at the burning ship, half of it now under water, it rushing in with the
sharks and flame. I nodded to her.

"Leap into the water." She said.

I ran across the flame and with one mighty push I leaped over the edge. I hit
the ocean water with a splash and Viviane gripped my Hand and took me
under the foam. As my head sank beneath the water, she kissed my lips tightly.
I looked up at the burning ship under the swirly glaze of the ocean surface. It

halfway submerging to the locker. I looked into the eye of the mermaid, and for some reason did trust her fully. I took her hand and she began to swim at surprising speed, her silver tail cutting specks through the silvery moonlight. I sank into the blue with Viviane, as a lifeless fish, becoming one with the deep.

To be continued....

CPSIA information can be obtained
at www.ICGtesting.com
Printed in the USA
FSHW022033050220
66869FS